BIBLIOASIS
TRANSLA

General Edito

YOU WILL LOVE WHAT YOU HAVE KILLED

YOU WILL LOVE WHAT YOU HAVE KILLED

KEVIN LAMBERT

Translated from the French by

DONALD WINKLER

BIBLIOASIS
WINDSOR, ONTARIO

First published in 2017 as *Tu aimeras ce que tu as tué* by Héliotrope, Montreal, Quebec.
Translation copyright © Donald Winkler, 2020

FIRST EDITION

Library and Archives Canada Cataloguing in Publication

Title: You will love what you have killed / Kevin Lambert ; translated from the French by Donald Winkler.
Other titles: Tu aimeras ce que tu as tué. English
Names: Lambert, Kevin, 1992- author. | Winkler, Donald, translator.
Series: Biblioasis international translation series ; 31.
Description: Series statement: Biblioasis international translation series ; 31
Translation of: Tu aimeras ce que tu as tué.
Identifiers: Canadiana (print) 20200228617 | Canadiana (ebook) 20200228706
ISBN 9781771963527 (softcover) | ISBN 9781771963534 (ebook)
Classification: LCC PS8623.A48393 T813 2020 | DDC C843/.6—dc23

Edited by Stephen Henighan
Copy-edited by John Sweet
Text and cover designed by Zoe Norvell

Published with the generous assistance of the Canada Council for the Arts, which last year invested $153 million to bring the arts to Canadians throughout the country, and the financial support of the Government of Canada. Biblioasis also acknowledges the support of the Ontario Arts Council (OAC), an agency of the Government of Ontario, which last year funded 1,709 individual artists and 1,078 organizations in 204 communities across Ontario, for a total of $52.1 million, and the contribution of the Government of Ontario through the Ontario Book Publishing Tax Credit and Ontario Creates.

PRINTED AND BOUND IN CANADA

The Last Judgment presents itself to each of us in the course
of our daily lives, no one is mindful of it and yet
here we are, this is the Apocalypse.
CHLOÉ DELAUME
Une femme avec personne dedans

A lying, hypocritical society turns around the grave
of the holes in the garden of childhood.
KATHY ACKER
My Mother: Demonology

PART

ONE

STEREOSCOPY WITH A FELT PEN

The teacher enters the classroom. She's wielding a cane
and her ruptured authority, the old witch, we're in grade
two, we're laughing at her behind her back. Her name is
Madame Marcelle. We make faces, make fun of her, play
tricks on her, but when she's eyeing us, we hunch back
down over our sheets of paper. The art room always makes
us nervous, I don't know if it's the colour of the walls, or
the drawings the other classes have stuck up everywhere
and that we peer at intently, to find them ugly mainly, and
mainly to read the artists' names so we can tell them at
recess they don't have any talent. In grade two we like
making art more than doing memory games, four plus
six makes ten, ten plus three thirteen, nine minus two six,
no not six, you're dead, go to the end of the line, no raffle
ticket for you to win that teaching game from Place du
Royaume, no neat new *Astérix* or *Garfield*, not for you the
stuffed animal you can keep all to yourself over the weekend but that you have to wash on Sunday because Jessica
Ménard's father complained to the teacher that the one she
got smelled: Simon Lapierre had it the week before and
when he brought it back, it stank. When the class found
out, no one wanted the *toutou*, the pet elephant out of

our French book that you can win for three days but that you have to bring back Monday, or Tuesday at the latest if you forget or if Monday's a holiday; you won't win it for sure if you get the wrong answer to the teacher's question when it's your turn in line, and it comes up fast. Sébastien Forcier made a joke when the teacher asked him his question, I didn't hear what he said, but the whole class laughed and me too. *Je dis, tu dis, il dit, nous disons, vous disez, ils disent ... non, **vous dites**, ils disent.* Go to the end of the line says Luc Cauchon, the snake-in-the-grass teacher who makes me copy out La Fontaine's *Fables* every Friday afternoon. In the art class Madame Marcelle, lifting her cane, commands: draw your house, the idea of your house, not your house but your *home*, where you live, what will be your memory of it one day when you're on your deathbed and you'll say to yourself: this house was my home.

Hard to take all that in when you're in grade two and Sébastien's hiding his Game Boy with its new cassette under the table, when Sylvie is trying to put pink crayon on your arms to say that you're gay because when you have pink on your arms that's gay. The stupid old stick of a teacher says: you're creating a disturbance. If we don't stop she'll get mad. She hands out sets of felt pens and sheets of paper big enough to keep us busy for at least three periods, each his own set, if you're missing something you raise your hand and Madame Marcelle will come to see you. The red and the black in my set are dried out, just like in all the other sets. They're always the first two colours to run out of ink, they're too popular, more than the others. Draw your home? You don't know what she wants, the dumb old biddy, we find it funny, she doesn't know why we're laughing, she probably thinks we're laughing at her and she's right. A house is where you live and grow and make lines on walls to show how tall you are. You hold up your roof like a beam holds up a roof, not forcing, free and easy, and going into the garage you write, in chalk, "home."

One sheet of paper, one only. We apply ourselves because there won't be any more, we get just one chance, nothing can be wasted. The house: its yard where we play in summer and freeze in winter, its lights that flick on when something moves in the black night, the lights that years later will betray us when we sneak home from the bar, go in through the bedroom window at the back, making no sound, the lights that reveal the red eyes we don't want our mother to see. The pop-up lights on the shed where we shut in Sylvie just for fun, just for a laugh in the dark, but Sylvie doesn't laugh, nor her mother, she calls our house and Sébastien's, and we get hell. The house, the road with its cracks and rainswept chalk, the black BMX tire marks left over from our very best skids. And the shifting sky, the sandbox dug down through the canvas that's been pierced by our plastic shovels going deeper and deeper in search of treasure, a tunnel to China, widening a fault in the earth's crust to drown in lava our Des Oiseaux neighbourhood and all the rest of Chicoutimi. The house, its swing anchored in cement, we don't push too hard so as not to swing over the top, the two tall firs, the green grass, the porch and the swimming pool where a cat drowned. I don't know how to start fitting all that in with my felt pen.

The cane lady sees me doing nothing and she raises her voice again, repeats that you have to put the cap back on the felt pens or else they'll dry up and make marks that come out pale when you rub them on the paper. We complain about the red and the black going dry, those are the ones we want most: the red because it's the colour of celebrations, of Mother's Day, of St Valentine's Day, of blood, of Christmas, and so on, the black for outlines, they're black, and you need to make outlines when you draw. Because my black is dry, I make my drawing without outlines, I tell myself that in real life there are no outlines, that when I look at a cat I see its fur, then the water in the swimming pool, with no line between the two, the cat and the water, the water and the cat, the cat drowned in the water. There are no outlines in my drawing, just beautiful big sweeps of colour that blend together, nothing closed off. Because he's pressing too hard on his pen, Simon makes a hole in his paper. Madame Marcelle says he'll have to fix the hole because she's warned us that we get only one sheet. Simon cries, and we laugh at him. The picture of his home has a hole in it, too bad, we'll see the wall right through it once it's hung up in the hall.

The green pen in my box doesn't work anymore. I raise my hand, Madame Marcelle comes to see me, I'm a dummy because I drew too much lawn, she shows it to the class, everyone laughs. I've wasted ink, I'm afraid she'll hit me with her cane, I make myself small in my chair. It's true that the lawn takes up a good half of the paper, but we have a big yard. She doesn't understand a thing. I hate her. I hate her so much that I want to throw a pair of scissors at her, poke out her little black eyes and squash them with my Warriors sneakers that light up when I run. The period's over, we've been goofing off forever, the old bat has thrown in the towel, she's sitting at her desk reading a big book. I get up and in front of everybody I shove a red felt pen into the big class pencil sharpener, turn it hard, and grind away.

The ink will spurt.

COMMERCIAL ADVANTAGES

It's beautiful, Chicoutimi, there's lots of broken glass and rivers wherever you go. A special place to grow up, really, with the blessed peace of its neighbourhoods: you can count on the person next door. There are dogs that bark at night, the smell of manure when the wind blows into the city from where it's spread over the fields in Laterrière. Beautiful parks. A bicycle path. Lots of conveniences. There are the lights on Boulevard Talbot, there's the Saint-Anne Bridge, green and rusted, over the wide, majestic Saguenay, you can cross it on foot, and oh! the pleasure. There are the neighbourhoods: Des Oiseaux, Desjardins, Domaine-du-Roy, the Quartier des Écrivains, Rivière-du-Moulin, Bassin, Centre-Ville and the Murdock, Côte-Réserve and the others, I don't know them all and I'm not going to do a Wikipedia just to describe my native city. There are also the parts outside, Chicoutimi-Nord over the bridges, and the other towns and villages: La Baie, Jonquière, Saint-Honoré, and so on.

You can find everything in Chicoutimi, whatever you want you can get at Place du Royaume, at Walmart, or the big Canadian Tire, or at Club Price going up Talbot towards the Parc des Laurentides. There's a great Rona next to Club Price, a big Club Piscine—one of the biggest. Or else there's Place du Saguenay, but there's not much left of it since Zellers closed, except for the hairdressers and the Laura Secord. Zellers was replaced by a big IGA, twice as big as the old one. It's funny, but it's as if people aren't going to the shopping centre so much since IGA moved in. Before, people went there to walk, they could spend the day there, eat at the Chinese buffet or have macaroni and cheese and a soft drink at the little Zellers restaurant, get an ice cream cone at Laura Secord, but since it's become a grocery store people hang around less, they just go to buy food and often the car is loaded down when they leave. Sears, at the other end, is doing pretty well too. The IGA on one end, Sears on the other, and the Chinese buffet between the two, which also does okay when it's not shut down for being unsanitary.

Our food stores can't be beat. It's true that the Bay closed down with its really neat Maxi, but in Chicoutimi we have at least two Metros, a couple of Intermarchés, a big IGA, a big Loblaws, a Maxi, a Super C. The Corneau Cantin too, but they're expensive and are always on the verge of going bankrupt. Still, when you get your Publisac at the beginning of the week, you can find good bargains. There's also Tanguay, which isn't bad, a huge Gagnon Frères with an escalator, the Bureau en Gros, an Omer DeSerres, all the dealerships (except for luxury cars), three

Tim Hortons, soon to be four, a super Pacini, where you can make your own toast, a Casa Grecque with a salad bar, a Scores with a nice salad bar too, a great new Jean Coutu across from the other Jean Coutu, but twice the size; in fact we're up there with just about anybody, even people in Quebec City. A great Winners, a Pennington, an H&M that's coming soon.

I grew up in the Des Oiseaux neighbourhood, behind the Place du Royaume, not far from the Rivière-du-Moulin park. When we were out of bread or milk, the IGA was as close as the corner store. That was before it moved to Place du Saguenay, where Zellers used to be.

RÉJEAN-TREMBLAY

The bell is ringing in the Réjean–Tremblay Elementary School, it's recess, we'll finish our arts and crafts in the next class. I wouldn't know how to describe this school, but it doesn't matter. We all remember our elementary school: where there's no place for bad words, no place for rudeness, watch your tongue, no place for the Tamagotchi you got at Christmas, no place for the Pokémon cards you trade at lunch hour, no place for candies in your lunch and things with peanuts that can give you allergies and that can kill people like Simon who has his EpiPen in his bag, no place for the Swiss Army knife that Amélie's father brought back from Switzerland, you leave that at home. Everyone has their space in the classroom where your name is written down on a piece of paper at the start of the year, and in the hallway where your locker has a little cardboard apple with your number on it, so you can't mistake it. At noon we each have a little chair around the school's daycare table where you eat your cold lunch in silence, otherwise you're sent off to eat along with the handicapped in the handicapped room, and you don't want to because you're not handicapped, your friends laugh at you and say you're gimpy, that you're a retard, even if they know it's not true, it's just a dumb punishment from the stupid woman in daycare, but it makes you feel sick to eat with them, they drool, they make noises, they can't feed themselves on their own, they have to be washed by a teacher, it's revolting. In the line you insert yourself between Sébastien (taller than you) and Simon (shorter), you do it fast when you're on the way out for recess, slower when you have to come in for the next class. You take your time before the free period Friday afternoon, you know you're going to spend it in the psychologist's office because Luc Cauchon's going to send you off to copy La Fontaine's *Fables* again, and you don't understand half the words.

They teach us all sorts of stupid things at Réjean-Tremblay School. They boil down the meaning of life for us and make us swallow it in little pills to calm us at lunch or when the nurse comes to see us and meets us privately to deliver her messages: don't trust anyone you don't know, get vaccinated, this is how to brush your teeth, my-body's-no-body's-but-mine, beware of Halloween candies where old perverts have hidden long poisoned needles that will send you right to your grave, you have to inspect them and throw away anything suspicious. They teach us to conjugate verbs and to get a grip on the world, they teach us the planets and the parts of the body that we can all check out in the gym's locker room. In music class we learn the do-re-mi-fa-sol-la-ti-do, in English class we learn phrases and songs, *Hi my name is Linda I'm a nurse, hi my name is John I'm a fireman, I love my job, hi my name is Peter I'm a student, what is YOUR name? What is YOUR job? Hi my name is Natalie I'm a teacher and I don't give a fuck, I learned English during a travel in Ontario, I learned English in school because there is more job as an English teacher, I study to become an English teacher because English is more and more important, you can go anywhere in the world when you speak English! Hi my name is Sylvie I'm a cat, hi my name is Anne-Louise I'm a princess, hi my name is Simon I'm a fireman too, hi my name is Julie I'm a doctor, hi my name is Sébastien I'm a serial killer, this is really funny, I don't understand it but I laugh* because everyone is laughing. In the grade two art class they wanted to make us think we were drawing people, homes, sandboxes, with a felt pen. And we believed it. A felt pen doesn't draw anything, any more than it can be sharpened. A felt pen is there to roll along the floor and make the old teacher slip, bring her down onto the stone slabs and break her hip. She has projects for us. Lots of things for us to draw.

SYLVIE FORCIER

Sylvie is a healthy child with a bright future who, one beautiful snowy morning, steps out of the house to build herself a fort. She's happy to see all this whiteness falling from the sky and blanketing her traffic circle. In grade two, I'm doubtless on the other side of Rue des Roitelets and the footbridge that leads to the rest of Des Oiseaux. Sometimes I cross over it to go and see Sylvie, but that morning I'm elsewhere, maybe at Dolbeau, or at the Saint-Félix chalet. But let's get back to Sylvie, who sees a big pile of snow left there by a truck, a mountain in the middle of the traffic circle and partly blocking it, she can hardly wait to jump into it, with so much pleasure awaiting her. Sylvie lives at 2008 Rue des Tourterelles, she knows the address just as she knows her telephone number is 418-696-2282, that the police are 911, and the ambulance is 911, that she's left-handed and that in her grandmother's day left-handed people were beaten until they bled. She knows how to count to a hundred and she also knows that she has to double-knot her sneakers, that she mustn't talk to strangers, mustn't answer the phone at 2008 Rue des Tourterelles when she's alone, must never say on the phone that she's alone, must never tunnel into snowbanks because a snowbank can collapse onto a child and kill her. There she is, at the door of 2008 Rue des Tourterelles, and she's going to play outside. Opening the door, Sylvie lets out her little cat that she loves so much, a lovely little cat with yellow eyes for whom she'd like to make a shelter in the snow so he can hide there and keep warm, a little house with a bed, a couch, a kitchen, and a snow toilet where he can attend to his needs. All primed for plunging into the brand new snow, she's put on her mittens, passing her hands through her jacket to be sure the snow doesn't get in, pulled her snow pants over her boots whose wet liners she's changed, pulled on a scarf and her Louis Garneau toque with three pompoms, she's ready and now she sees it, the big pile of snow beckoning, left behind by the plow.

AN ASSIGNMENT

I'm in grade two, and Madame Marcelle and her cane are teaching all the groups in the school. I'm in Group 2B with Sylvie, Sébastien, Simon, Anne-Louise, Marc-Antoine, and lots of others, we're laughing our heads off at the gimp, we call her "Cane-Cane," or "shitty pissy turd," the more obscene we are, the harder we laugh. Before leaving Friday for the weekend, Cane-Cane says: during your holiday, go and see your grandfather or your grandmother— or take a photograph if they're dead or too far away—and draw them in your notebook. She gives us that assignment, the putrid piece of shit, because we've been too disruptive. They'll be really happy to see you, they're all by themselves in their old folks' homes, they're ancient, from another generation, another era, they're signing out, they already have one foot in the grave, talk to them about their time, hurry, talk to them about their youth, talk to them about the good old days, draw them the way you see them, blah blah blah.

They're disgusting, old folks' homes. Simon's grandfather is there, and it seems he smells, he's dirty, and all the old guys grab at you, and they have rotten teeth. Back in school on Monday morning, I draw, on my notebook page, a kind of elongated half moon. Madame Marcelle knows my grandfather, he's the former school principal. She knows that he doesn't look like this white thing that covers most of my page. She gets real mad when she asks me what I'm up to, and I tell her that it's obvious, it's a ghost, it's perfectly clear, anyone would have known that. Madame Marcelle gives me a bad mark.

FERNAND THE GHOST

In elementary school we always have a week off at the end of winter, the worst time of year when the weather is never sure of itself and the school's child care service is closed. My mother works, she doesn't have time to deal with me, she looks after Sylvie and doesn't want me to come along because we always argue, she doesn't want me to stay by myself either because the last time I set a fire on purpose, so she sends me to stay with my grandparents in Rivière-du-Moulin. I've always hated this boring neighbourhood behind the golf course, over the bridge on the way to La Baie, you turn left at the light, a place where there are beautiful trees, peace as far as you can see, good well-off people who take their cars and go to work without being a bother to anyone. A serene neighbourhood where there's never a murder or a rape or anything like that, nothing so compelling that we're going to hear about it on the news or in a newspaper, none of the treacherous things that go on in Montreal especially, or in the downtown apartment block where all of Chicoutimi's criminal element is concentrated. In a neighbourhood where I have no friends and don't want to make one, I'm stuck spending the day with my boring grandparents who make me do drawings while I watch TV. They've bought me some new felt pens and I have to pretend to be happy. They've made me a bedroom in the basement, down stairs that creak when my grandfather Fernand descends them at night to pay me a visit and make me swallow what he has to offer. It's ugly, my bedroom, I have a bed that's too big, with the oldsters' old comforter, and it smells all over of the potpourris my grandmother Ruth collects like a nutcase.

On the second day that the school is closed, my grandfather gets out of bed and imagines he's going over to "the Other Side." Setting his foot down on the ground that day, he's overcome by a feeling that eludes him, an unfathomable intuition, bereft of logic but vehement in its certainty, that he is seeing things from a different perspective, through a new filter, and, who knows, that he's saddling his old ankles with less weight. It's something strong, enormous, unerring, like an isolated shower or the truth in a Chinese fortune cookie, like a punch to the gut that feels good, that shows you you're only the ghost of yourself. Ruth is upset by his strange behaviour. She calls my mother, tells her how he's playing the fool, that he thinks he's invisible, that at every turn he insists that objects are levitating as he holds them up in the air to try to frighten us. My mother understands nothing, she hasn't got time for such nonsense, she hangs up the phone. Ruth becomes angry with Fernand, wears herself out telling him that he's not transparent, that all she can see is an old fool who is waving her potpourris around in the empty air and scattering them to the winds. But Fernand takes his task seriously, and insists on mimicking the behaviour of the best ghosts he's seen in the movies. At night he hides in the back of the closet to startle me. I take fright, Ruth is disheartened, she leads me off to sleep with her and locks Fernand in the basement bedroom. The next morning we go down to let him out. I follow my grandmother with my nose pressed to her dressing gown, the stairs creak, and we understand nothing: Fernand is on his feet, a sheet over his head, in front of the door to the still-locked room, we don't know how he got out. When we go near, he raises his arms gently and starts to make ghost sounds. My grandmother takes away the stupid sheet and puts it in the wash, leads Fernand up to his room, and lets me play all afternoon.

It's hard for a ghost like Fernand to haunt a neighbourhood so partial to life, so remote from all cemeteries, so isolated from a direct and daily contact with death. People in Rivière-du-Moulin don't take well to poltergeists and their kind. We bury them quickly, our dead, in Chicoutimi, so as to hear no more from them. Ruth eventually goes along with Fernand's mission from beyond the grave, she even ends up every night ironing the white sheet he wears on his head to go wandering through the neighbourhood streets. Once, I ask to go with him, but Ruth won't hear of it, there's no way she's going to send an eight-year-old child meandering through the streets in the dark with an old lunatic who thinks he's a ghost. One night, towards the end of the week, I wake up because I hear a noise overhead. The police are in the doorway with Fernand, handcuffs on his wrists and the white sheet around his neck. He had decided to haunt the neighbour's house, the neighbour hadn't liked that at all, he'd freaked out and called 911, my grandfather was lucky not to end up at the police station, he could have been fined or even sent to prison, you don't walk into people's houses like you do into a church.

The weekend arrives, I go back to living with my mother, but Fernand continues to haunt and torment us. His otherworldly delirium goes on, and Ruth refuses to commit him. Later I will be faced with his phantasmal madness every day, when my mother dies and I'm forced to go and live, until the age of twelve, with my grandparents at Rivière-du-Moulin. It's the night when I'm getting ready to move on from elementary to high school. I'm used to my grandfather's excesses, but dark days are in the offing. After several months of bloody diarrhea, Ruth dies in her turn. Fernand, despite his ghostliness, is devastated. The old man probably thinks that, in dying, Ruth will join him as a ghost and together they will be able to haunt their house and those nearby. It doesn't happen. Ruth doesn't survive her death. Nor does Fernand: one day a white ghost is seen throwing itself off the Sainte-Anne Bridge to shatter on the Saguenay River ice. He has left no explanatory letter, as is expected when you take your life. In the spring he is scooped up and buried along with his ubiquitous white sheet, in the Chicoutimi cemetery, in a hole near that of his wife and their daughter, where immense green toads will arrive each night to reproduce around their graves.

SNOW REMOVAL

It's Sunday morning and a fine snowfall is dusting the traffic circle on Rue des Tourterelles. The cars are parked in their driveways, snugly plugged into their block heaters so they'll start on Monday morning, otherwise you'd have to call the tow truck and risk being late for work. On a weekday morning the traffic circle would be swarming: parents on their way to the office or the factory; small children waiting for the yellow bus at the stop on the corner of Rue des Hirondelles; older ones taking the city bus a bit farther on, at Rue des Roitelets; those in college or university travelling in their own cars or those of their parents (the less fortunate among them standing at the bus stop along with the high school students). But on this Sunday morning all the houses on Rue des Tourterelles have the uneasy appearance of the morning after a family tragedy, when the delivery man has not yet arrived to see, through the front door window, blood on the white hallway walls. Nothing newsworthy has yet taken place on Rue des Tourterelles, but whoever was there on this January morning could sense a tragedy in the making.

A door opens at 2012 Rue des Tourterelles, a man comes out, seems to be in a hurry, wearing jeans and big boots, an undershirt under his unzipped coat, his toque just now plunked down upon his head. A plow hired by the rich families to clear off their private driveways has already opened a path and left an enormous pile of snow that blocks part of the traffic circle. Kevin is one of the crew of Robin Morin Inc., responsible for snow removal in the neighbourhood, and he's late. He has to blow this mountain out of the way before he gets another complaint. Sunday he works only if it's snowing, and this morning it is snowing. Except that Kevin had a big night last night, he went to bed late and got up early, with a girl he didn't know in his bed. The girl didn't seem to be in a rush to leave. They stayed facing each other at the kitchen table, Kevin already had his coat on and was doing everything he could to appear restless, jangling his keys, tapping his foot, checking his watch over and over while she ate her toast. Tired of waiting, he left, telling her to shut the door behind her. Kevin Lambert hates clingers who believe in transcendental concupiscence, or, in other words, love. He never forgets that love is above all a carefully constituted cocktail, well mixed, served to a girl in a bar, the offer clear, the promise substantial. The girl who has awakened between Kevin's sheets this Sunday morning is still tipsy from the drinks bought for her the night before. What the girl doesn't know is that the man she has slept with is a murderer, or at least that he'll become one in a few hours.

What the man doesn't know is that the girl with whom he has spent the night is only recently a girl, Paul become Paule, just back from having one of her body parts transformed, from the installation of a brand new sex organ in a successful operation carried out for very little money in a clandestine clinic in Cuba.

Kevin jumps into his car to go and get the snow blower at the garage, forgets to unplug, takes off dragging the cord, stops, gets out, yanks it free, rolls it up, sets it down near the front steps, gets quickly back behind the wheel, reverses, checks the rear-view mirror, and brakes hard: his little neighbour Sylvie is there, just behind the bumper. Chilled to his boots, Kevin opens the door, exits, tells her to be careful, tells her it's dangerous to play behind cars, especially when they're turning, that she might have been run over and that would have been terrible. Sylvie is awkward in her big bright snowsuit, she moves away, falls to a sitting position on the snowbank, and starts crying because she's been bawled out and her cat is under the car, she wanted to take it out of there and it went into the motor. No Sylvie, cats are afraid when cars start, it's too hot in the motor for a cat to breathe, the cat's gone away for sure, cats are 'fraidy cats, it must be somewhere in the traffic circle, not very far. With a wave of his hand he leaves her alone with her distress, and drives away.

FIRST DAY

On the first day of grade one we already know how to write our name, it's one of the things we learned in kindergarten, things we were judged on that weren't constructions or Lego boats that you hid away so your rare pieces wouldn't be stolen. In grade one I'm in Madame Isabelle's class, she passes around cardboard already cut out, pale-yellow cardboard you can decorate with drawings of things you like, if you like dogs, you do a dog. We get out our new pencils, the pencils we have to buy that are on the list of school supplies, only those will do, the same Prismacolor wooden pencils with our names on little labels so there won't be any arguments.

It's an individual assignment, but this is the beginning of the year and we can talk. The desks are in rows, one in front of the other, but we can get up to look at what our friends are doing. On the pale-yellow cardboard we write our names in beautiful big coloured letters and I do that too. That's how you're going to learn it because I haven't said it yet. Faldistoire, it's written the way it's said, F-A-L-D-I-S-T-O-I-R-E, it's not often you can get it right on the first try. Faldistoire, you don't see that very often, is it French? French from France? Faldistoire

Beauregard on a pale-yellow cardboard that's going to be stuck onto the front of our desks so Madame Isabelle can put names to our faces, she'll learn them fast, we're going to spend the year together.

At the beginning of the year the classroom is empty, the walls are almost all white. We'll be decorating them all year long. The walls are going to fill up, they'll be colourful as springtime, all covered with our gorgeous projects. Except for the wall by the door that's filled from floor to ceiling with vocabulary, with words, gentle words, innocent words, they don't want to teach us just yet to read what we shouldn't. No words about violence in the world, the world's imminent end, or about people who jerk off into skulls, no words about cancer the silent killer, or the darkness that sometimes wells up within us and draws us to the chair and the rope—hanging yourself as a fuck-you to the world—no words about wars, no word in this vocabulary that tells the truth about our earth chock full of dead bodies, whose slimy soil has been oozing death since the world began, where you can no longer push in a shovel without extracting some human scrap, some corpse from some slaughter out of some unremembered genocide.

When we've finished our handiwork, we go to see Madame Isabelle, and she gives us some Scotch tape to stick it onto the front of our desks. Anne-Louise has stuck hers on upside down and when she pulls on it to unstick it, it tears and all the sparkles fall off. Her pale-yellow cardboard is torn and she cries, she's ashamed and cries harder, it's the first day of school and we're not comfortable enough yet to laugh our heads off, we have to look respectful, we hold ourselves back. We can't help comparing our projects with Madame Isabelle's example. Hers is always the nicest. She's prepared it the night before, at home, with her husband or her girlfriend, they do exist, homosexuals, like little Pierre-Luc who cries all the time and talks like a girl, you have to be nice with him, just as you do with the handicapped. He's on two legs and his chair is rocking, he always does that, balances himself precariously on the two back legs of his chair, he knows it's forbidden, that it's dangerous, he's often been told that it's dangerous, but he never thinks about it. No one in the class knows that a pencil holder can be deadly, that's one of the things we learn from Madame Isabelle in grade one. Anne-Louise's HB lead pencil is pointed right at the ceiling. Pierre-Luc loses his balance and falls backwards right onto the pointed lead, he gets up quickly and the whole class sees Anne-Louise's Star Wars pencil sticking out from his skull, we start to shout but Pierre-Luc howls even louder, Madame Isabelle says don't touch! Don't touch! She's taken a course in first aid and she knows you mustn't remove a foreign object that's buried in a skull that's still soft. The class is cancelled. Pierre-Luc is taken away in an ambulance while we're left sitting in the gymnasium, doing nothing.

TO JR IN JONQUIÈRE

Thanks to our family connection, I find pictures of Paule before her operation in the photo albums of Angèle, my grandfather Fernand's sister. He had been her golden boy before he was disowned by the whole family because of his transsexual lunacies. When you eat at my great-aunt's and, a bit tipsy, she starts talking about her only son abducted by the demons of sodomy because his father was never there to discipline him and to alert him to sexuality's most twisted vices, I pretend to go to sleep on the couch and I listen to her song and dance as she curses a life that always gives all good things to the same people, Mother Nature who makes families of ten children without a single one that's fucked up, while my great-aunt is there all alone to shovel the shit of the entire world. Angèle, my grandfather's sister, is a defeated, alcoholic woman, ostracized by the small community of Canton-Tremblay because she herself must have sinned to have given birth to such a creature. My grandmother Ruth feels sorry for her, she has a big, sensitive heart and she's full of empathy for her sister-in-law, it must be terrible to have brought into the world a child who has betrayed us like that, personally she would rather have had a deformed infant or one that was stillborn. In grade two I rummage around in Angèle's basement while my mother and my grandparents eat and drink for hours, I look at all the old albums with the plastic pages stuck together, the names written right onto the pictures in black pencil, I open the dusty boxes full of old birthday cards. On the photos there is Paul as a boy at different ages, at the beach, at the cottage, in the schoolyard. Not one taken after the age of twenty. It's just that in Canton-Tremblay you don't say, "I like boys," in Canton-Tremblay you don't say, "You've got the wrong person," in Canton-Tremblay you don't say, "I'm not a man," in Canton-Tremblay you don't think you'll be happier with a different identity, there's not even any transvestism in Canton-Tremblay, or if there is—there's the former mayor who, every night after his wife died, wore her underclothes while stroking himself with her pearl necklace—you hide in the basement with the blinds drawn to be sure the neighbourhood kids don't spy on you and go broadcasting it to the whole wide world. That's what happened with the mayor: his career ruined, his house vandalized. Everything sexual is deeply repressed in Chicoutimi and its surroundings; out of fear that our children may become unbalanced and end up displaying their private parts in the daycare's windows—that's already happened—we'd rather not take any chances, and it's not one of our subjects of conversation. Except for weird incidents: those, we want to know about. We like it when they're talked about on the radio or in *Le Quotidien*, or when we learn about them from the neighbour across the fence if it's not something being discussed in the media: like when a kid in nursery school is caught down on his knees in front of a grade sixer in the woods behind the school; or when a father who's taking care of his daughter all alone at the cottage has taken advantage of her, the old pervert; or when Anne-Louise and Sébastien heard their parents having sex and told us about the noise they made. Sex in Chicoutimi is mainly something that goes on in the basement, when you get up at night without making any noise, and you open your computer to jack off to hard-core penetration, bareback, interracial, pussy, twinks, fetishes, fists, BDSM, lesbian, group sex, role play, daddies, teens, trans, miscellaneous. You pump yourself up with pleasure, handkerchief by handkerchief, while checking out the little neighbour's Facebook page, then you delete your history as if nothing's been going on.

In a Jean Coutu Photo Centre envelope, I find what I'm looking for. Someone who didn't know what had happened to Paul probably thought the pretty girl in the photo was his sister or his cousin. It's poor quality and backlit, there are two copies that I steal from my great-aunt Angèle. One day my mother finds one under my pillow while she's making my bed, she orders me to come downstairs immediately, I swear that I've never seen the picture I stare at every night when I go to bed to try to understand how the young boy I've seen in the albums, the one with the fishing rod on the cottage dock, a trout in his hand, smiling ear to ear beneath his *Gilligan's Island* hat, could turn into this girl with hair like a girl and a real girl's dress. Yet she seemed happy as a young boy on his first day of school, with his teacher and his new lunch box. My mother confiscated the only known photo of Paule, post-operation, before sitting down to tell me this horror story, that's what she said, this whole business was a horror story, Aunt Angèle wouldn't want to know that you've been going through her photos, she's trying very hard to forget all the bad times she's been through. Viviane educates me, takes the time to explain to me the violent episode of the first surgery, botched, of the second, success-ful, under the distant palm trees of a troubling island in the middle of the ocean, where the water's so deep that you can't go swimming and where you can be eaten by sharks. She takes pleasure in telling me her horrible story, and paints a portrait of Paule by showing me the Devil in her tarot deck, the fifteenth card, half man, half woman, who chains up little children and subjects them to all kinds of abuse. She burns the photo in the fireplace, these are not things to put into a young person's hands. As it happens, I'd hidden the duplicate in my book *Tales from Around the World*.

I swear that on this photo that I cherish, Paule is a very pretty girl. To pay for her operation she even went to work at JR, in Jonquière, the only strip club in the city of Saguenay, where my father, fearful about my being drawn to the male member, would take me much later to vaunt the charms of female curves being rubbed up against a stainless steel pole. Sometimes I fall asleep with the photo in my hand, and in my dreams Paule dances clothed in only the thinnest of veils. Paule, the secret poison seeping into me as it seeps into the beer mugs of the men who've come down on their motorcycles from Arvida to witness her transcendental disrobings and the mystical swaying of her hips. I read the future in Paule's movements, Paule who calls herself Kim Dragonne at JR, a ridiculous, ugly name like those of all the other dancers. When she dances, for a moment I know that what's coming is dark and terrible, Paule is the physical prefiguring of an approaching end, of an end in progress, perhaps already consummated in part, she bears within her sex the transerotic eschatology of Chicoutimi; unhappy will be those who do not know how to gloss her clairvoyance. There is no place in Chicoutimi or its surroundings for people like Paule, who is forced to work, to pass herself off as a whole woman before the end of her operation, and to be a source of anxiety for many clients, afraid of being faced with the unwelcome surprise of a sexual revelation they hadn't bargained for. The JR receives many complaints on that score. She is devastated by it.

What Paule is oblivious to is the hypocrisy of the complainers, the number of pornographic films rented at the video store every day, featuring women of her type; girls who are not really girls, who exist in the to-and-fro of physical and sexual identities, in the no man's land between man and woman. Paule invalidates all the existing classifications in the moronically categorized "XXX Films" section of the video club where I work while going to high school. For more than one Chicoutimi resident, it's a source of fascination and compulsive masturbation, a body like hers; I've washed the spilled sperm off the DVDs. You wouldn't have believed me, Paule, if I'd told you that many a trucker would like them for himself, those implants, that scar at the base of the penis. You let me see it during those dreams that returned to me night after night. It's your signature. You've come back from the dead to haunt my most beautiful nightmares. Show me your scar. It's so long . . . You have guts, you're tough, you're terrible, Paule, you scare me and teach me what's beautiful, you charm me like an opened bottle charms an alcoholic, but above all dance, don't stop, because the night is coming to an end. Dance, Paule, exhaust yourself while you're spinning and spinning about, pass your hand around my waist again, one more leap, one more step, Paule, I want to be the drop of sweat that rolls down behind your ear and down your back. You're short of breath, it's hard to do what you do. But do it; only then do you make everything clear, do your intimations of the end infuse Chicoutimi's foul air.

I never attend Paule's mystic dances, except in dreams, listening to my grandparents and Viviane talk during the long meals when they try to console Angèle for her failed life and her ignoble son. But I see her every night, as she dances non-stop. She plays a role in my favourite Play-mobil as a pirate on which I place a long Lara Croft tress of hair, in film scripts I invent in my basement bedroom. I see her as the heroine she is, and seek her out when I go to see the dancers with my father. One day she will die: for her I will go and cleanse the cemetery's earth before the interment of her cast-off body. In the slough of the excluded where fetid green toads thrash about, I will lay myself down.

MACHINES MURDER CHILDHOOD

Kevin is on his way back to the Rue des Tourterelles aboard his deafening monster, speeding through Des Oiseaux: the machine's metal squeals loudly when the snowplow passes over a hole in the frozen asphalt. He's well into his twenties but looks sixteen, he reminds you of those teenagers on television sitcoms played by actors who are much too old, you tell them to drop their pants below their bums, put their hats on backwards, you give them skateboards so they seem to have come "right out of high school." You can sense Kevin's hairless chest under the jacket he's wearing in the truck's heated cab, it feels like a furnace in there, but he's kept his toque on to free his face from his long blond hair. Before starting work he lights a cigarette, looks at the big pile of snow he has to clear, an iceberg in the middle of the street, it's dangerous, it will block the road when people are leaving for work or coming through the traffic circle. Kevin doesn't know that in a few minutes little Sylvie, buried there, will be torn to pieces by the blower's sharp-edged screw, turning over mechanically on itself, gobbling everything in its path. Sylvie is buried in the snow and it's a real shame: children do not always have the wisdom to respect even simple instructions. Even if she knows she lives at 2008 Rue des Tourterelles, that her right hand is on the right, her left on the left, that she's left-handed and that in her grandmother's time left-handed people were shut up in cages beside the road and left there to be eaten by horrible black crows, that you mustn't take candies from strangers, not say "Marie noire" three times in front of the mirror, that you have to listen to Viviane when she tells you to go to bed, that you must never tell the truth on the internet, even on the game sites where you've made a friend, because this friend is certainly an old man who wants to do all sorts of things to you that you can't talk about at school, even if Sylvie knows all that, excited as she is by the snowfall, she may have forgotten that you must never tunnel into a snowbank.

Sylvie's tunnel is exquisite. She's dug it right at the bottom of the pile, and it goes in deep. Her idea was to cross through it from one side to the other. But her architectural skills are limited, and it collapses as soon as she enters it. Sylvie is trapped, stunned by the weight of the snow dropping so heavily onto her little body that's cocooned in a thick snowsuit. She tries to move, but she can't, she cries with her little voice, snow is weighing on her mouth, her nose, her eyes, her entire body, it's cold, she turns on one side then the other, she tries to dig herself a path, push away a bit of snow, she manages to find a little hole for her face where she can breathe without swallowing ice. She is able to cry a little bit louder, but around the traffic circle nothing can be heard but the low-pitched growling of the snow blower. The packed snow smothers the little high-pitched sound Sylvie is making. Her hands are trapped under her body, her thumb is twisted inside her mitten, she tries to turn her head, she tries with all her strength to move her feet, but the snow is too heavy.

The snow blower is coming, Sylvie, you'd better move. Do you hear the machine? Maybe you think it will take away the snow and you'll be able to escape. You hear the blower turning, sucking up the snow to spit it out farther on, into the centre of the traffic circle, near the street lamp: you're afraid. You cry, you cry some more, you yell, and your little tears run down your cheeks. It's dark. You swallow snow when you open your mouth to cry out your distress, but all your sounds are smothered, they don't reach past the hard lumps that are holding you down in the depths of Chicoutimi. You don't know what to do, you're suffocating, you push with all your body, but nothing moves, you're angry, desperate, deafened by the growling motor, the mechanical shovel. Its pistons are making the whole street shake, are pounding the ice-hardened ground. Exhausted by your efforts, you grow calm for a moment. It's there, Chicoutimi, everywhere around you, it has swallowed you up in its snow. Think, you have to get out of this fix, otherwise you'll never have the two dollars for the tooth you lost this morning that's sleeping on your pillow. Cry, Sylvie, cry that you want to see your papa and mama again, your little cat and the Mickey Mouse posters in your bedroom, howl that you want to be babysat again by Viviane. Hammer this black snow with your feet as hard as you can, fend off the cruel mechanics of the snow blower, insist that it's not its decision to make. The pitiless snow is obliterating you, Sylvie. You give a few feeble kicks, then you stop, frozen stiff by winter. Out of strength, of breath, of courage, your voice is lost beneath the grumbling of the snow blower, beneath the heavy layer of snow. In despair, you murmur, "Marie noire" three times. You hope to call up a spirit, an avenging ghost, a soul in pain, you want to sell yourself to the devil for the rest of your life, if only to carry on a little bit longer. Even the evil spirits have abandoned you. The blower spits out a brief jet of scarlet snow, with Sylvie pulverized inside it, onto the snowbank.

Soon the whole city will learn of your death. Your mother will weep for a long time, will break her favourite knick-knacks and her prettiest framed photos of you. Your coffin will be buried in the Chicoutimi cemetery. On your grave will be carved a little Mickey to remind you of the posters in your bedroom. And the vile toads will come, every night, to sing in your memory.

THE DEATH OF THE NOTEBOOK

On Monday morning, in the residential neighbourhood, Sylvie is at every family's breakfast table. You see her mirrored in cups of cold coffee, on the front page of *Le Quotidien*, in the children's cereal scattered about, you hear her crying through the hairdryer's din. You go to school, to the office, and at a street corner or a traffic circle, seeing a snow blower in action, you wonder if it's there that the accident happened. Her blood is leaking out still. It stains my notebook with its perfectly round, perfectly red drops, falling onto blank pages in our grade two classroom, where I miss her, my friend by default. She and the cat, I draw them with a felt pen or in watercolour, a big red blot bursting onto the body of a little girl, a cat all blue and stiff, frozen into shiny powder glued onto the page. It's "my project," pinned up for a few weeks in the administration hallways along with all the other class drawings and the banner *WE WON'T FORGET YOU SYLVIE FORCIER*, in honour of our dead friend. I wonder if Sylvie still exists. I'm troubled by the question of her body. I want to know if the status of a dead person is changed when the body is utterly pulverized. Her blood is still mixed in with the watercolour on absorbent paper, pinned up in the administration's corridor. It's the first time I have gone to the end of that hallway. I didn't know what was behind the closed door at the very end, with no window to see inside: a room where you closet Sylvie's parents, my mother, Viviane—who seems to be the most shaken by the tragedy—and me, to do psychology on our brains and make sure that we won't go right out and hang ourselves. It seems like this will be hardest of all for my mother.

Sylvie has already been back to school for several weeks. It's very strange for us, in the midst of mourning our friend, to see her again one morning sitting alone in the empty classroom, there before everyone else. Sylvie carries on as if nothing has happened. The yellow cardboard with her name on it has been thrown away, she makes another one during our math lesson. She also, like all the students, makes a drawing in her own memory so it can be put up in the corridor. Sylvie draws herself dead beside the big snowplow, even if, despite her tragic demise, she's still among us.

HERE LIES

Faldistoire. Sometimes I think I own the most ridiculous name anyone could come up with, the name my mother gave me for some still-obscure reason that I've been pondering for a while now, seeking a buried meaning, perhaps one that doesn't exist. I console myself, thinking that I might have been called Kevin, and Kevin is even worse. Kevin conveys banality, implies indifference. It suggests the shed at the bottom of the schoolyard where they leave you for fun one afternoon, just to get rid of you.

For a long time Kevin Lambert was traumatized after having killed the child Sylvie. Exactly nine months after the accidental murder, a girl he slept with one night, just like that, coming back from the bar, gave birth to an offspring: his. This girl, as we know, is Paule. She wants nothing to do with a child, but decides all the same to fully assume her maternity, an experience that will perhaps take her mind off the phantom penis she still feels between her legs. A doctor, for reasons having to do with her pelvis and pain, strongly advises against a natural childbirth. He also recommends terminating the pregnancy, as a precautionary measure. She refuses. Paule carries the child as one carries a placard during a demonstration, not because she loves it or lends it any importance, but in order to express herself, aiming a stiff blow from a truncheon at nature's exposed ribs. The body she so hated ends up being her downfall: she splits in half on the floor of varnished two-by-fours where she gives birth. The child is saved, Kevin Lambert inherits it, a heavy responsibility for an ex–snow clearer with no right to unemployment insurance, who has put his house up for sale on the internet. He buys his son a little cloth outfit, black, at Mode Choc, for his mother's funeral.

Paule is buried at the very back of the cemetery, in the spot where you relegate all those who have no right to coddled paths and greenery, to flowered and ornate graves, those who do not deserve to share a space with the respectable dead of Chicoutimi. They use her savings account to pay for a fairly nice plot. A sculpted angel rises stiffly above it, its gaze empty, its wings stretched wide. An angel that's praying, but no one can say, given its sardonic air, if it's sincere. In the vicinity of the grave are those of a Jewish family, three Protestant families, a few criminals, and the excommunicated, all neatly hidden in the shadow of mighty oaks that connive with the poorly cut grass to conceal them from the eyes of visitors.

For a time my mother takes me every week to Sylvie's grave, where she sheds hot tears. Sometimes Sylvie herself goes with us to the cemetery while my mother adds flowers to the plot. The little girl is bright for her age, and she understands that death is hard to accept, even when the departed in question comes back to a life she continues, for a while, pursuing. She supports Viviane in her mourning, helps her to honour her own memory. Sylvie is buried in the spring, a few months after the accident with the snow blower, as soon as the mild weather melts the frigid winter's last snow, allowing the green grass to revive on the ground into which the gravedigger's shovel sinks itself. The cemetery is full of people. The extended family, friends, neighbours, schoolteachers, the mayor, the owner of the Robert Morin snow clearing company, all have dressed in black and come out to share the sadness that goes along with the lowering into the earth of a small coffin, to be embraced by the welcoming arms of Chicoutimi's dark earth. Sylvie herself is present for her own burial, while people sadly lament her loss on this beautiful spring day when I am in grade two.

I remember being bored by the interment of my friend by default, by my mother's melodramatic behaviour, weeping loudly, breathing heavily, fanning herself with both arms, pretending she is going to faint, being just unsteady enough to have herself comforted by strangers. Tired, I go for a walk to give myself a rest, stepping over the new grass, its growth encouraged by the spring sun and solutions of 20-20-20. I imagine the dead bodies decomposing beneath my feet, even if I know that they are being protected from the worms in their aluminum-lined boxes. In the cemetery, with its varied tombstones, its paths with their asymmetrical bushes, I very quickly lose my way; my mother departs, leaving me there. Too shaken by Sylvie's burial, she lacks the courage to go looking for me in the farthest reaches of the property, and tells herself that this will teach me not to wander off. The sun sets over the mausoleums, the gate closes upon the tomb-strewn domain where I will be spending the night, alone with the dead bodies and the weirdos who come here to masturbate. A cold green toad, like those you find among the rare four-leaf clovers growing at the feet of graves, comes to perch upon me.

BURIALS

All funerals are the same, one buried body is much like another, the dead are interchangeable and eternal. The day when Sylvie is left behind in the cemetery's depths, I have a prophetic vision of my mother's burial. The nights are cold in spring, and Viviane has left me stranded among the deceased. I cry for a while, try to scale the fences with their large protruding prongs that might, if I straddle them, spear me through the groin, as happened to Romy Schneider's son. I go to sleep surrounded by the chilly vegetation of my childhood cemetery. I am in Chicoutimi, but I am elsewhere too. In the dreariest moments of a dark night all cemeteries are one, and the dead who speak to me are from Témiskaming, Trois-Pistoles or Montparnasse, from Saint-Henri to Santo Domingo, from Notre-Dame-des-Neiges and Batiscan all at once. This night I am not in Chicoutimi, I am wherever the earth extends a serene welcome to its cadavers, but rarely in good faith, there's almost always a knife hidden behind a back, a blade brought out as soon as the sky grows dark, the better to cut the cords binding the defunct to his demise, not to mention the perennial toads that on every night known to the world leap about among the black crosses and the dandelions busy feasting

on human flesh. Forgotten, alone in the shadows, I curse
Viviane and Sylvie. On my hands and knees in the muddy
grass, before the grave of someone unknown, I read my
mother's name. My own as well, small and black, in letters
almost totally worn away, which say *FALDISTOIRE*. I will
swear on the heads of all whom I've known that I saw, in
the depths of this long night, my name carved on a stone.
I fall asleep on the grave that is to be mine.

Viviane never really had a sense of timing. She takes
Sylvie's death very hard. Several months after the accident
with the snow blower, when I am sure she isn't thinking
about it any longer, she kills herself. Her farewell letter
is a giant "Im goin to mis Silvi," scrawled with a pencil
she must have had some trouble holding in her hand. My
mother has once more, this year, forgotten my birthday,
because on the October day that I come home from
school with my cardboard *Toy Story* hat, I find her hanging in the kitchen. An expert knot suspended from a hot
water pipe has proved to be too much for the pipe, split
open by the force of Viviane's body dropping from the
chair and swaying about, with her hands at her neck, as if
she regretted having acted so soon. She is as beautiful as
an onstage angel afloat thanks to some intricate machinery,
she is a guardian angel descended from heaven thanks to
some clumsy special effect, a two-bit illusion like those
that dazzle the more gullible spectators in a theatre. On

the table, her letter, five words. Just beside it, a big bucket of Gagnon Fried Chicken from her favourite restaurant, and a few greasy wipes. She'd offered herself one last treat before her demise.

Viviane babysat Sylvie during our whole childhood. After the death of her little *Vivie-my-love*, as if to repent for a non-existent sin, my mother began inviting her to the house every week. She made her cakes, rice pudding, which she knew I hated but made on purpose, she served her tricolour ice cream and took her to Gagnon Fried Chicken. As a child, I had Sylvie as a friend by default, but after the day of the snow blower, when she was totally pulverized, something changed in her.

The ghosts . . . The dead, I mean. You mustn't say "ghost" because it's a bad word, like saying "fairy" for a homo-sexual, or "cripple" for someone who's handicapped. The dead who come back, those from my childhood I spend time with, have something different about them when they return. It's the same for Sylvie and the same for Pierre-Luc, who also went back to school shortly after his skull was pierced by a pencil point. It will be the same, soon, for Sébastien, my best friend. My mother, for her part, died for good and never came back.

At her funeral I lose the name Faldistoire and become The-Son-of-Viviane. Her boy, her only son, he has the same face, he has her eyes, she didn't find him under a toadstool for sure, her only child, my condolences, what's your first name? Faldis . . . what? Faldistoire, that's unusual, that's beautiful I mean, Faldistoire, what does it mean? Open the dictionary, you stupid idiot . . . Why that name? My mother has left with her secret intact. Taking refuge in the bathroom to escape the embraces and the smell of hairspray, I think again about Sylvie's empty, closed coffin, and my mother crying all the tears out of her body. It seems so long ago . . . I know that Viviane would have been sad to see that Sylvie wasn't there for her own funeral. All afternoon, while the anonymous faces file past, the powdered cheeks jostling each other to kiss me, the handshakes, too firm, the strong perfumes and that, nauseating, of the flowered wreaths, I think of Sylvie, and of the mortuary tribute in our art class notebooks.

In her grave, my mother is wearing her favourite dress and a bouquet from a broom plant. We bury her as the flowers are beginning to fade, the day after the funeral, in the Chicoutimi cemetery, right beside the graves of Fernand and Ruth, her father and mother, in whose house I am now going to live. The cold buffet in the living room amuses me. Just before her coffin is closed for good, just before sending her off to burn to a crisp in the bowels of the furnace, I slip in a few chicken sandwiches. The priest asks me if I want to throw on the first handful of earth. It's sunny in the cemetery. It isn't raining, there are no black crows, night is not coming on, the sun is there, the sky is blue, and no one, certainly not me, would say anything to the contrary. In my backpack I have the sketchbook with the drawings of my mother and Sylvie. Before the undertaker completely buries the urn, I bring it out and drop it into the hole. No one notices my occult ritual, my prophetic gesture, except the gravedigger, who doesn't give a damn. He finishes burying my mother along with the sketchbook on which my name is written. I imagine it going to seed, bad seed in the soil of Chicoutimi, spreading afar, reaching away, putting out roots everywhere under the earth. Already my future is set down without my knowing it, without my being able to read it to correct the mistakes in grammar and spelling, the errors in logic that ought to be expunged from any narrative; my life and its tale are planted in the earth, already foreknown, decreed, determined, in this notebook where I drew my home.

I stay on alone with my grandparents when everyone has finally gone. My knees are stained by the damp earth and the green grass, just like when I fell in the backyard of the house in Des Oiseaux and my mother bawled me out because of the grass, it's hard to get out in the wash. Leaving the cemetery to go to the parking lot, we follow a little dirt path bordered by trees. Along the way I see Paule's grave. The statue of the angel paid for by the money she earned with her body, dancing with a stainless steel pole in her hand or a biker's shaft in her mouth, has already been vandalized. Her praying hands have been torn off, her wings as well, the angel can no longer fly, her empty gaze and the smile at the corners of her mouth now seem despairing. No one has gone there to weep or to lay down flowers. No one, except for the black crows that wait for the toads to come out before diving earthwards and swallowing them whole.

SEEING RED

He's a notorious madman lunatic, Luc Cauchon, a super sickie, a rapist, a pedophile, there's a space reserved for him in the prison downtown, but they've never caught up with him, hidden as he is behind that ridiculous name, Luc Cauchon, and his absurd role as a grade two teacher. In his hands he holds a big white Jonas pet store bag that by the way looks pretty heavy. It's the last day of school, there's a pile of report cards on the teacher's desk. We've come just for that, to receive our report cards and say hi to our friends, also to those we can't stand, those to whom we don't really talk for fear of being hassled by our friends, the real ones, we're saying goodbye to everyone one last time because we won't see them all summer. Sébastien didn't turn up for his report card. He's left on vacation with his family, they're in the south, in Maine, on the beach at Old Orchard. He always talks to us about Old Orchard, Sébastien, the word sounds Chinese, it's really cool to go there, it's not Quebec, it's the United States, there are beaches on the ocean and awesome amusement parks, you pay with American money. In class 2B we've never seen American money, we know the United States is pretty close, you can get there by car. Sylvie thinks Sébastien is having us on because to go to another country you have to take the plane in Montreal, five hours down the road from here.

On the last day of grade two we can sit wherever we want. The cards with our names on them have all been pulled down by the caretakers, the walls are empty again, there are no more drawings, no themed pictures from our French workbook, no more creations from our art class. The pictures of our friend Sylvie, freshly dead, the mortuary tributes we had to compose with our felt pens on absorbent paper, are returned to us along with our notebooks by Madame Marcelle, who comes by with her cane to wish us a good summer and to tell us how nice we all are. For one last time she says whatever comes into her head, sure of herself and with an old crackpot's silly grin, it's all bullshit, we know we put her through hell, she's trying to soften us up so we'll be kinder next year when we take her class again. Sylvie looks down at her notebook, at the memories she recorded during this poisonous year. I'm right beside her, we're waiting for our report card and the raffle, that's what the tickets are for.

Luc Cauchon puts the big Jonas pet store bag down on his desk. It's a surprise, something extra for the draw, we're all super excited. On the last day of school for grade two, the pupils in class 2B who've been good in class, who've learned their games and their verbs by heart, have a chance to win a snake. A live snake in a little box with holes in it, bought that morning at the Jonas pet store by our teacher Luc Cauchon, who thinks it's a good idea to give us a little live creature, that taking care of it will show us how to be responsible. Simon starts grumbling and I don't blame him, he says that's shit on a stick, a little reptile like that. A dog or a cat would be a lot better, a poisonous snake or a big tarantula, that would be much more cool. Luc Cauchon doesn't agree, he doesn't like a negative attitude, even on the last day when you'd think everything would be allowed because you're maybe never going to see him again. We're still in class until the end of the day, he's the one with power, and he removes Simon's tickets from the draw—the year ends badly, he can't win anything, he blames himself for having such a big mouth, curses Luc Cauchon under his breath, rattles his desk just to make some noise. The first ticket has Anne-Louise's name on it, the lucky stiff, of course, she always wins everything, all the time. We're happy because she chooses the pottery kit that nobody wants anyway. Sylvie picks up the *Garfield*, her second-favourite comic, because *Astérix* has already been taken by Marc-Antoine. She's happy to have one all to herself, a beautiful new comic, and not to have to fight during library period to get those still on the shelves, the ones she's already read and that aren't funny, all old and ragged. The prizes go fast. The twin wins a gift certificate in a bookstore, Luc Cauchon makes a joke about his bad marks in French, everyone laughs except for the twin who's ashamed, now, of his prize. Sébastien would have won one of the three snakes, but he's not there. Lots of us haven't won anything. He has his hand inside the name bag, does Luc Cauchon, we're all focusing on his fingers as they unfold the paper, it's silent in the classroom. When I see his face as he reads the last winning name, I know right off that it's me, I can see how it burns his ass to give me a prize (he still hates me for the petition I drew up, demanding that he be fired). Against his will he pronounces the word Faldistoire, and I find myself the owner of the last snake.

Not long after the bell rings to mark the end of our second year, we're freeing the snakes onto the concrete in the school playground. I send mine down the spiral slide, that makes Sylvie and Simon laugh, especially when it falls onto the cement slab full of sand that awaits us at the bottom of the slide where we can twist our ankles and crack our skulls, our teachers put it there hoping for a serious accident that might brighten their day. It has grains of sand in its eyes, my snake, on its body, on its tail, it's wriggling around and we're doubled up laughing. Faldistoire, you wouldn't dare crush it with your sandal. I do it, to the hilarious laughter of my friends. Anne-Louise pulls a little cloth bag out of her pottery kit, hands it to me, and tells me to put it inside, that would be fun. I shove my snake in, it bites me with its little teeth, I get mad and close the bag. My finger is bleeding, the whole class is around me, laughing to beat the band, and clapping loudly as I move towards the school's wall. I whack the bag twenty times on the stone, until my hands are blue from holding it, until the snake's stopped moving entirely. Before taking the bus, I get it out and bury it in the sandbox. I make the sign of the cross and leave it to its infernal lot. Soon the summer's gulls will come to dig in the ground with their beaks and will rip my little snake apart.

PART

TWO

VANDALS

The teacher says: draw your house, the idea of your house,
not your house but your home, where you live, what will
be your memory of it one day when you're on your deathbed and you'll say to yourself: this house was my home.
I take the brown crayon, I draw a rectangle with a sort of
perspective, the back of the house seems to float in the
air. To correct my mistake I make a lawn with a green
crayon to fill the hole between the house and the horizon.
That makes it look as though it's leaning forwards. Sylvie's
a whiz at drawing. Sometimes other kids in the class ask
her to draw a castle, a cat, a backstreet boy, drawings they
give to their moms and dads saying yes, I did it myself. And
Dad can't see a thing, he has cancer and he's going to die,
everyone thinks Sébastien is too young to understand, but
he understands. We understand too, in the schoolyard, the
secret going around: Sébastien's father is dying. We don't
know if we should be laughing at Sébastien or pretending
that nothing is happening.

Yes, Sébastien, I'm up for sticking a felt pen in a pencil
sharpener. Yes, Sébastien, I'm destructive enough to do it,
I'll show you and the other kids too. In grade two Sébastien is my best friend, but Sébastien's best friend is Simon,

or sometimes Charles. I get up, I go back around the big table, I walk to the middle of the classroom. The crazy old gorgon who's teaching us and whacking us with her cane is sitting at her desk. Me, I go just to the side, behind her back, I push the felt pen into the sharpener and I turn. The result is disappointing. I imagined the ink spurting, red all over the walls, on the floor, on my face. Nothing much happens, the pen stays stuck there, and the kids at my table slap their thighs hooting while Madame Marcelle, furious, drags me outside.

In the principal's office my mother is crying. Her words stick in her throat. Unable to line them up one after the other, she spews them out in a gravelly cough, spills her conspicuous overkill all over my guilty feelings, expelling it into her handkerchief in great desolate discharges. My mother performs her soliloquy, gives vent to her vehement lamentation, signs everything the principal gives her, and leaves the office dragging me by the wrist. I spend the evening in my room with nothing to eat: a serious punishment coming from her, who serves herself two plates of spaghetti as consolation for having brought me up so badly. The next day, Saturday, is her day off. But Sylvie's mother is working, and my mother is babysitting her daughter all day. On Saturdays I often have to play with Sylvie. If Simon knew I was playing with her, he'd laugh at me so hard that I'd for sure be out of the gang. Only Sébastien knows that Sylvie is my friend by default, but he's in the same situation: Sylvie is his cousin. Sébastien and Sylvie play in the same street, and when I have to go outside with her, I go and get him too. We have fun running away from his cousin, trying to lose her in the little wood behind the traffic circle, or making her eat the salt they put down in the streets for melting, until she gets a stomach ache and vomits. Sometimes it works better than others: Once, Sylvie spent one whole night in the woods because we tied her to a tree. Coming home, after managing to free herself, her teeth black from dirt, her eyes red and crusty from having cried too much, her nose snotty from her having slept in the dead leaves, she didn't tell on us. She's a good friend.

In winter my mother makes me wear the awful hat she likes so much. I go out with Sylvie and the cat to play in the traffic circle. We often take the footbridge where the older kids smoke in secret at five o'clock and we're on our way home to the other part of Des Oiseaux where my house is firmly anchored in the ground, not floating in the air like in my botched drawings. In summer, when I take the footbridge on my bike, I get up speed so as not to stop where that gang of older kids hangs out. I'm in a cold sweat and I pedal fast, especially when they start laughing or shouting something at me. Their faces are just asking to be smashed in, I hate them, and I'm afraid of the drugs they're smoking in long cigarettes, I'm afraid they have sharp knives or pointed needles they'll dig into my skin to make me sick even if I haven't done anything. By the time we get to Des Bernaches the snow's really coming down. Tomorrow the plows will push it away. In our part of town, they blow the snow out front. At Sylvie's, they blow it towards the traffic circle.

PSYCHOLOGY

One Monday, in his office, the psychologist wants me to talk about myself and I don't. I pose like for a photo in a magazine, my mouth shut tight, a big smile. When, frustrated, he brings his hand up to me, I bite him hard, and get a three-day suspension. I'm forgiven, but it's very hard, this mourning I've conjured whole hog, looking down from my nine long years. Because my life is riddled with death, everyone on earth is trying to figure me out. It all has to fit together, my problems with authority, my knee-jerk violence towards other students, my cruelty, my being good in school too: since I have social deficiencies, I must be compensating with my performance. Adults project their most terrible perversions onto my silences. They'll never be able to explain me completely, to get to the roots of my thoughts, there are no roots and there's nothing to think. I hope they'll make themselves crazy trying, that I'll drive them all to suicide, that I'll force them to plant bombs, to drink blood, to set Réjean-Tremblay School on fire.

CANCER AND ITS INCONVENIENCES

Sébastien doesn't understand why his grandmother, who has come to babysit him and his sister for the weekend, wants to tell him something serious. Sébastien doesn't care, he just wants to go back to beating Marie-Loup at the Nintendo she got for her birthday. He doesn't want a conversation, especially not with his grandmother Madeleine, who's talking to him as if he were an adult because he's old enough to understand. With her tender little looks, her hands on his arms to keep him listening, and the stress she places on certain words, she's treating him like a grown-up, yes, but it's a grown-up retard she's addressing. What's she up to, the old lady, she thinks she's his mother. She's a pain. Sébastien likes Madeleine when she does what she's there to do: give him presents or take him on holiday to her trailer in Saint-Gédéon. Up yours, Grandmother, he'd like to say, as he does sometimes to Simon or me in front of the whole gang to show that he's not afraid of bad words. He's not listening to his grandmother when she says that Papa is in the hospital and that's why his parents aren't there. It's happened before, anyway, when his sister was born, he remembers them picking him up at school and having him babysat until the following night. His parents came home with a little wailing baby, and he had to pay attention to it, not to think of it as just a thing even if the newborn didn't talk, didn't walk, did nothing useful except eat and scream and poop, hog everyone's attention, and all the gifts. Now he thinks she's okay, his sister. He's used to her. But he still regrets a little not having held her under the bathwater longer the day he tried to drown her just to see, especially when she starts going through his things, or his parents make unfair rules to favour *her*. His sister didn't yet know how to talk, that time with the bath, but now that she's big she can fight and cry, and tell on him too. There won't be another good time to smother her.

Madeleine is feeling bad for poor Sébastien, who's in denial and doesn't even look at her, he's sidestepping a cancerous reality with the Game Boy in his hands, madly tapping his unease away and not frowning the least little bit. She explains clearly, to her grandson, that his father's cancer is going to be hard to heal, that he'll be spending all his time at the hospital, suffering a lot, that he won't be able to make crepes anymore for supper Friday nights when Mama is working, that if things go badly he might never be able to make crepes again, that he'll be losing all his hair as well. It's better not to tell Marie-Loup, his sister, about this, she's too young to understand. It's all right, we'll get through this together, and if you're feeling bad, you must talk about it. Sébastien nods his head and saves his Game Boy match before going downstairs to the playroom. As soon as he opens the glass door, he tells Marie-Loup that Papa has cancer. She'd like to know what that is, cancer, but she's too young to understand.

His father's illness will in the long run be a boon to Sébastien, with everyone being extremely nice to him during the entire treatment period and beyond. Even if his father doesn't die and Sébastien doesn't get a penny of the inheritance he would have received if the cancer had worked a bit better, his sad situation leads to a remarkable social advancement for him between his second and sixth years of elementary school. At school, all the teachers are aware of the family drama afflicting the Forciers. It should be said that Sébastien's father was then a well-known figure in Chicoutimi: the mayor's right hand, active in all the local and educational committees, the owner of beautiful lawns, a former real estate agent whose photo on the placards outside properties for sale drew people's eyes, a man with sparkling teeth, well-coiffed, whose face would bring any mistress to a climax if he were unfaithful, but he was not, he made tender love to his wife, was a good family man, the first to get to his feet and applaud his son's goals in hockey tournaments, the first to whistle his salute at the end of a gymnastic show in which his daughter made awkward somersaults, and president of a charitable club made up of professionals from different spheres who had breakfast together every Tuesday morning at the Coq Rôti to discuss their next fundraising campaign and to sing happy songs, a fine friend to all those he knew, a friend who listened devotedly, ready to lend a hand to anyone at all, but measured in his involvements, reserved in the giving of himself. After his diagnosis, nobody could figure out how a man who was so healthy, who cycled thousands of kilometres every summer, who ate healthily and talked about it to anyone who'd listen, a man who, every morning, swallowed his little capsule of fish oil and his large glass of orange juice—and the imported nuts at noon, and the vegetarian dishes in the evening, and who ran up enormous bills at the natural foods grocery store—could end up with such a serious cancer.

RELOCATIONS AND MALEDICTIONS

Kevin Lambert's life wasn't all that rosy. If killing a child is never good for your reputation, killing two can be catastrophic. Kevin's child was born without a name, he called it Croustine without explaining why. After the Rue des Tourterelles tragedy, Kevin is demoralized. Fired by the Robin Morin snow removal company, finding himself in a precarious financial position, unable to endure the sight or the thought of that gloomy traffic circle, Kevin, ten months after the birth of Croustine, goes back to live with his father in Rivière-du-Moulin, behind the golf course. The day he moves, when all the boxes are in the van parked in front of 2012 Rue des Tourterelles, when young Croustine is already in the car seat, when his grandfather is at the wheel and ready to leave, Kevin pauses to breathe in for one last time the Des Oiseaux air. It will soon be autumn, the children will be back at school, I will doubtless be starting grade three in a few weeks, but that day maybe I'm at the cottage, or at the shopping centre with my mother, who will soon kill herself, or perhaps I am playing with Sébastien and Marie-Loup. Or I am at that traffic circle, right near Kevin, who is perhaps looking at me with his farewell eyes. Our ball will have rolled under the wheels of the moving van; casually, I'll have crawled underneath to retrieve it. Marie-Loup will be pedalling fast on her bicycle with its little wheels, one higher than the other, forcing her to constantly turn in circles. Sébastien, hidden behind the garbage can with his slingshot, would be trying to hit his sister. I've forgotten the day when Kevin Lambert left the neighbourhood. I have no memory of the afternoon or the songs of the birds throwing themselves from their nests, breaking their necks under the trees before being eaten by snakes. I'm talking about this very real day that exists nowhere in my memory because I must, the morning has ended, the afternoon is coming, and I'm down on my hands and knees on the asphalt, crawling along to find the ball under the truck, Sébastien is throwing stones at me, Marie-Loup has fallen from her bicycle and skinned her knee. Suddenly I remember the thunder, the sky going dark, the wind coming up, and the door to Sylvie's house opening.

She has lost her daughter, killed by a man who is now moving house. Sylvie's mother wants to sow chaos within Kevin's skull, to bury there a long white worm that will eat away at its insides and drive him mad. When she comes out and dark clouds cover the sun, I understand, down on all fours on the pavement, with Marie-Loup's tears as a soundtrack, that what's said about her is true. In the schoolyard, in the classroom, at the big table where we eat at noon, at the school's daycare, Sébastien has often declared, not too loudly, so that Sylvie won't hear, that his cousin's mother is a witch, that even his parents have admitted it. A real witch with powers, who concocts mysterious potions, who is known all over the world, who makes prophecies, who reads crystal balls and eats live frogs, talks to the dead, and lights candles without using matches. She is his father's sister, but they haven't talked for years. She's screwed up, she took drugs when she was young, and because of that she's gone off the rails. We sometimes taunt Sylvie about it, her witch of a mother, but at the same time we're all afraid that she'll cast a spell on us, that she'll be watching us in her crystal ball and that she'll put a curse on us from a distance, that she'll see us being mean and will change us into grasshoppers or even worse, that she'll kill us, make us disappear, turn us into vegetables like the children in the handicap vehicles at Réjean-Tremblay School, you never know with people like that. We believe in her mother's dark powers, especially since Sylvie gave a speech about what she does, and since we've read *Harry Potter*.

Sylvie's mother is called a haruspex and is a real witch, she tells the future as well as the past, the known and the unknown. Sylvie said so in her presentation in French class where we had to say something about our parents, to boast about them and show how interesting they were, to persuade ourselves that they weren't total failures like the rest of the Chicoutimi population. There are jobs that are cooler than others. Simon's father is a union representative, everyone slept or drew pictures during his talk: dull as dishwater. Anne-Louise's mother works in an office, she does accounting and files tax returns, she spends her days with rows of figures on the ninth floor of a building, we found that very high but frankly didn't give a hoot. Anne-Louise would have liked to talk about her father, but he's a biker, that wouldn't go down well in front of an elementary school class. He sells drugs all across town and has long swords hanging on his walls as decorations, but they're kept sharp, his decorative swords, in case someone breaks in at night to cut his throat or shoot him with a gun. Ornamental weapons to defend yourself for real. Pierre-Luc's mother is an archaeologist, a kind of Indiana Jones who cleans off arrowheads with a little paintbrush, who digs up Native treasures buried under our parking lots, the remains of an old Algonquin village. She finds shells, necklaces, tools, objects they used every day before the cowboys savagely killed them off with their hunting rifles, like we saw in *Dancing with Wolves*. As for Sylvie, she was a real hit with her talk about her mother, who's known all over the world, as you can tell by her bilingual website, when you go there you have to choose "French" or "English," she travels a lot, she leaves for entire weekends to go and predict the future in the United States or Montreal, stars come to see her sometimes to have their cards read or to adjust their auras, apparently Céline Dion consulted her and she predicted everything she was going to become.

So the moving van is loaded up, the car also with little Croustine inside, ready to leave, the sky grows dark and the wind comes up at the traffic circle. The Des Oiseaux haruspex comes out onto her stoop in a dressing gown, one stiff finger pointed at Kevin Lambert, on whom she advances. The street's dust and leaves are swirling around the enchantress; I see everything, crouched under the van. That morning the haruspex invokes all the arcane forces to pronounce a curse on the new father. I find it magnificent from where I am, grandiose and powerful, her black hair billowing in the wind. Her eyes are flashing, she's shouting words I can't catch, magical verbal assaults, and the girl in the pile of snow, and the accursed boy, little Croustine, all are one: out of it comes a terrible wish, a prophecy yet to be realized, a curse that she flings towards Kevin while spitting in his face and slapping him before turning on her heel and slamming the door of 2008 Rue des Tourterelles.

Two years later, when he will have almost forgotten that strange moment, that crazy lady who said so many mad things, the curse will come true: on a Tuesday, at the Saint-Félicien zoo, as she'd predicted.

JESSICA'S EGOTISM

In our grade two class there was a little girl called Jessica who was born I think with a problem in her joints that made her calves bulge out from her body. I don't know if there was a connection, but her right eye also wandered, and seemed, when she walked, to be in sync with one of the calves in its awkward waddling, I don't remember which one. I do remember that Jessica missed a lot of school days every year due, I think, to her medical appointments, and all the pupils hated her for no good reason because of her frequent absences, made even more obvious by her leaving right in the middle of a mathematics or French class. In grade two, knocks on the door are enough to drive a class crazy, so that Luc Cauchon has a lot of trouble carrying on with the lesson afterwards, and has to shout into the ears of the most keyed-up among us in order to calm them down. We get very agitated when someone knocks on the door during a class: Perhaps someone is there to announce that class is cancelled, as happened the previous year because of the sewer backup into the locker room, it was the fault of the twin who had blocked the toilet while trying to flush down his exercise clothes. Perhaps the pastoral care lady is coming to talk to us about the old gentleman who is always wandering near the school with a stroller full of vegetables, vegetables injected with drugs that he sells to families in the neighbourhood. It happened to Simon's cousin the year before, he ate a carrot and it made him vomit and see spirits. A whole family was even poisoned to death after eating an onion that he'd sold them, according to Sébasse.

Every time that pounding on the door resonates through the classroom, Group 2B comes to life, only to be deflated more often than not, seeing Jessica's parents or the secretary telling her that she can gather up her things. Jessica gets to her feet to leave, and the hatred directed her way comes to a head. A remark on her deformity launched brazenly in the direction of the barely closed door, an imitation of her orthopaedic walk by Anne-Louise, pretending to go and toss a piece of paper into the blue basket, the class's nastiness provokes gales of laughter on all sides every single time, giving our teacher Luc, merry as a mortician, much to contend with. In addition to the privilege of all those afternoons off, the little tart gets special treatment from all the teachers. Those imbeciles who sate their lust for power by intimidating eight-year-olds all flip over the cripple. Towards the end of the year the whole school is sitting on the floor of the gymnasium, which amplifies the echo of all the groups refusing to shut up. The principal is at the front, struggling to make himself heard, he shouts for us to be quiet, but we're caught up in our games, our laughter, the rumours we're sharing regarding the pupils in the other classes. It's the day for handing out school prizes and for the grade six show, a stupid play they've worked on all year long and are going to proudly present, with their we're-older-than-you faces, so the whole school will find them super hot and envy their talent, their self-confidence, their skateboard shoes. We, our gang, with Sébastien and Anne-Louise and Simon and Charles, we don't give a shit about them, we make fun of them just like we do the others, we're ready to fight them even if they're bigger: we'll hit harder. The gala begins, and our teachers give out prizes to the smartest students in each grade, the ones who are most adored. Not too bright, the grade two teachers have decided to give almost everything to Jessica Ménard, so she has to get up every five minutes to go and collect the awards for Academic Application, Athletic Application, Personality of the Year, Academic Performance, Good Behaviour, and so on. Every time her name is called, she gets up with her big gummy smile to go and show off in front of everybody her new clothes and her beautiful Mixmania T-shirt, and it's an intolerable injustice to see her walking off with all these honours while lots of normal students could just as easily have won a certificate and the movie tickets that go along with it. Halfway through the gala, Jessica has enough winnings to go and see four or five movies, and the sneaky laughter, the sarcastic remarks whispered into our neighbours' ears, no longer suffice to channel our resentment. And so Sébastien makes a move, edges his way cautiously down to the first row, and trips Jessica just as she's about to rob us of another ticket. Her deformed, clumsy legs are of no help in regaining her balance, and she falls headfirst onto the flooring with its painted lines for one sport or another. The room goes silent. We hold our breath, seek out others' eyes. Then it all explodes, every class in the school starts to howl with laughter before the spectacle of Jessica's rout, even the grade sixers, despite their maturity, even the nursery schoolers who laugh without knowing why, seeing what their elders are doing. As of that day, Sébastien, who suffers no consequences thanks to the sickness gnawing away at his father, becomes the most popular student in the school. He makes five or six friends in grade six, and we all envy him.

BICHON

Raised by his taxidermist grandfather, Croustine is happy clambering all over his collection of stuffed animals, imagining himself living real adventures on the backs of real animals in real imaginary lands. Kevin finds himself a job as cook on a James Bay work site. One evening he comes home with a little dog, a young bichon that had belonged to an elderly couple in the neighbourhood. When Croustine sees the cute all-white dog for the first time, he is delighted to at last own a real live animal, climbs onto it right away, and breaks its hip. Unlike stuffed animals, living creatures do not have a solid wooden structure under their fur. On the living room carpet, the poor bichon, its rear legs paralyzed, howls and bites Croustine's ankle, and he kicks it in reply. Kevin comes running and finds the poor bichon all broken, and his son in tears. Croustine explains as best he can that the dog bit him, he shows the blood on his leg, he weeps from shame, from pain, having damaged his brand new dog, he's assailed by a stew of feelings hard to sort out at such a young age.

The veterinarian tells Kevin that he would have to entirely reconstruct the doggy's hip. The cost would be enormous. When the little boy is put to bed that night under his dinosaur comforter, the little bichon is given a meatball laced with rat poison. To console his grandson, the elder Lambert applies his gifts as a taxidermist to a beautiful pair of slippers, with at the toe of the one on the right the little dog's head, its tongue out, looking to the future.

A month later, his two hands glued to the window of a house in Rivière-du-Moulin, young Croustine is waiting. His grandfather has told him to watch for the arrival of a delivery truck and the boy is determined to obey. It's a surprise, a present for his birthday, he mustn't miss it. In the basement, Grandfather Lambert is inserting a glass marble into the eye socket of his latest creation. Every day he spends several hours refining his sculptures of flesh, feathers, hair, and scales, coming upstairs each evening with a new species. Some might find it strange to preserve so many dead animals in one basement, a sort of taxidermist freak show, an exhibit of cadavers all laid out, something that might seem repugnant, but to pass that sort of judgment on the old man would be to discount his tenderness, the care he takes in his work, carefully extracting all the usable parts of the creatures, salvaging nature's wreckage that, otherwise, would be lost to memory and to the gullets of scavengers. For anyone who can appreciate a dead animal, the elder Lambert's basement is a gold mine, a treasure imbued with a taxidermist's wisdom, where a variety of canny stagings faithfully reproduce nature in all its wild beauty. Lambert's basement is a veritable museum where taxa and species, an aesthetic sense and *savoir faire*, come together to produce fine art.

Soon the grandfather will be torn from his work. Young Croustine, excited by the arrival of the van, runs down the steps as the delivery men are depositing in the living room an enormous box with many customs stickers, containing the specimen of which old Lambert has long dreamed: a genuine African lion, in one piece, its jaws open wide, one paw perched upon a block, with imitation sand and dried grasses underfoot, all arranged with remarkable attention to detail. Croustine cannot at first believe his eyes, and shrieks with joy, climbing onto the back of this monster that supports his weight much better than the little bichon he is now wearing on his feet.

THE ORANGE HALLWAY

The handicapped hallway is located between the two wings of Réjean-Tremblay School: the first where everything starts out, where you find the kindergarten classes, grades one and two, the day nursery, and the gymnasium; and the second where you have to go to reach the music and art rooms, to find the secretary's office when you're sick or the principal's office when you're a revolutionary, or to make your way towards the mysterious, nebulous realms on the second floor that are home for the third, fourth, fifth, and sixth grades. I've never gone that high, but it appears that if you're not at least in grade four and you go up there, you're given dirty looks, and grade sixers once shut a youngster up in a broom closet just to scare him silly. It also appears that the drawings in their hallways are beautiful beyond belief, that they go for recess there without having to get in line, that the teachers are really strict but that sometimes they take the whole class out at noon hour to eat at McDonald's.

The normal students rarely go into the handicapped corridor. When you do navigate it, it's with the whole class, in line, between periods, when the classroom doors are closed. You don't often meet up with the six orange-coloured classes, the handicapped don't go out at recess or eat at the same time as we do, they have their own hours, a bit different from ours so we can't mix, so they won't contaminate us with their sicknesses or attack us (because there are some who are really crazy, a big retard once jumped on Anne-Louise for no reason and we all wanted to smash his face in). As for me, I go back and forth along the corridor's orange walls, often going alone to the school psychologist who makes me copy out a hundred times that I have a problem with authority. I take the opportunity to peer in, through the windows, at what's going on in those classes that so disgusts the other students, taking care not to be caught by a specialized ed. teacher or an orthopae-dist who might sound the alarm, shouting at the intruder. Réjean-Tremblay is known for two things among the young people of Chicoutimi: for the coloured rectangles on its facade and for the many students in special needs classes. I often say, when I'm playing hide-and-seek with the neighbourhood kids, that I go to Félix-Antoine-Savard, otherwise I'm called a retard who goes to a school built from Lego, I hate that so much, it makes me feel like punching people in the face.

The first kid I was in love with and to whom I gave a bloody nose with my fist as if to make him pay for his beauty, his muscled body, his hold over my gaze, that was on a street in Des Oiseaux, behind two big fir trees in the yard behind my house, our hiding place. His name was Almanach. He was a grade one in my school, a younger kid whom I often saw in the corridor where the lockers for grades one and two face each other. I was drawn to his nonchalant air, his bashful smile, the jokes he made under his breath and that everyone went quiet in order to hear, his discreet and sarcastic sense of humour that pleased even the older kids, even those in grades five or six, who found him really neat for a youngster. I was drawn to his dark skin, like an affront to Chicoutimi's latent racism, his black hair and eyes: a long, stiff finger thrust deep into the anus of our charming city, goading it on to a powerful and involuntary climax. I liked the aesthetic effect of our names side by side: Almanach and Faldistoire, two impossible names, but which melted into each other, as fluid as a hand descending to the elastic of one's Batman boxer shorts, where you can gently insert a finger, then another, in a slow exploration of the possibilities of our underdeveloped bodies. Almanach Boivin, his mother had chosen the last name, his father the first. His parents are crackpots who study rocks at the university, who bang them with their hammers and peer at them through their magnifying glasses, who seek out gold and diamonds, his father even came from Morocco just to hammer the Chicoutimi rocks, it seems that some of them are really special, but it's going pretty far to start eyeing a bunch of gravel through a microscope. Almanach

Boivin with his strange two-headed name in the fourth year of high school, a name mottled like an arched back with its pale scars etched into his skin, part of a stunning change that is plain to see in the locker room: Almanach has grown at least a foot between grades nine and ten. My love for him began with the orange hallway in grade two of elementary school, and my heart broke in grade three, on the first day of school, when I didn't see his black fore-lock anywhere; Almanach had moved, changed schools. I no longer saw him behind the fir trees, where I had bashed his chin with my knuckles before running off, I no longer hid out with him, no longer squabbled with him at that game we'd spent our weekends playing. I found him again in high school when he entered the Lycée de Chi-coutimi at the same time I did, having skipped a year, given his dogged intelligence, somewhere between grades four and five. I penetrated him at the crack of noon.

All of this was already there in our stupid games; my fierce second grade punches set the stage for the furious hip thrusts in our intoxicating lovemaking. In the orange corridors of Réjean-Tremblay School, the hallways of the deformed and the retarded, those unfortunates despised by nature, I make my way slowly towards my afternoon of writing down words while the rest of the class plays at tfou.com, Clue, *Pokémon Yellow* on Game Boy, Magic cards, lovecalculator.com, Harry Potter The Game on the computer, or other stuff I don't do, I'm on my way to gaily copying cicadas and ants, wolves and foxes or other fables, carefully chosen by Luc Cauchon so I will reflect on my behaviour in impenetrable old-style French. The handicapped corridor is deserted. It's Friday afternoon, they're on one of their frequent outings, doubtless at the college swimming pool. Nobody, not a single pupil or teacher. I go into one of the rooms. It looks like a normal classroom: big tables, games, construction materials, a TV with *Cornemuse* cassettes—that shitty show they made us watch in grade one, I've always said it was for morons—letters and numbers on banners, but one thing that's different, something you don't find in any of our classrooms, a kind of enclosure at the back of the room, and a thick blue mattress that's all soft, with cubes, spheres, and other geometric forms made of sponge. I can't quite take in what's happening at that point, but for some reason or other Almanach comes into the room. Almanach, thanks to the love marks I'd given him on his jaw or on his eye whenever I had the chance, has managed to find me on a dark, rainy afternoon during a boring free period, lost somewhere along the orange corridor. He enters the classroom where I'm lying on the mattress eyeing the holes in the ceiling, turning them into constellations. I remember his shadowy, dark eyes in the bluish half-light, I remember the rhythm of the rain drumming on the sidewalk, rinsing away the chalk drawings, the hopscotch games, the anonymous declarations of love. Almanach joins me in that room on the orange corridor without saying why or how he's found me, and lies down on the mattress. We're seven and eight years old and something like tenderness, a knife planted in the midriff, one damp hand in the other, locks of hair just brushing each other, all swim together. Faldistoire, we have the same favourite Pokémons, we know the words to the same songs by heart, we're both waiting for *Harry Potter 3* to come out in French, I've read them too. I've put on my Batman boxer shorts and I know he's wearing the same.

SÉBASTIEN AT THE COTTAGE

My grandfather Fernand has a cottage near Saint-Félix-d'Otis, where he lives with Ruth from June to September. After my mother's death, when I'm living with my grandparents full-time, I have to spend my whole summer there. Far from the day camps where there's a circus program or a swimming program and where the monitors are super hip, I'm bored to death, so my grandmother Ruth gets me a friend to play with, but only outside the house. The two of us spend most of our time making plans to get back in unseen or to burn the house down. Once it almost works. I'm with Sébastien. He knows quite a bit about fire, he knows you have to build it up, add newspaper and little twigs, he gives me a stick lit at the tip and when I put it down on the cottage windowsill, the foam insulation flares up right away. The fire crawls up inside the window, but it doesn't last long, just long enough to scare Ruth and Fernand, who run out and extinguish it with a pail of rainwater. We start to feel bad as soon as we see the family rush out, especially me, I don't really know what to do, I hide behind the shed. Ruth sees us and we're given what for just as if we were dogs. After, in my bedroom, we do imitations of my angry grandmother, who looks really weird with her hair in the air, spitting, and that vein bulging out of her neck that makes us think she's going to die right in front of us, because of her blood pressure. Despite the fix he's put my family in, Sébastien returns the next weekend, because his father is sick and he's a bit upset, and we have to help him take his mind off things.

My grandfather loves it when I have friends over. I'm not allowed to sleep in the same room with them because Ruth surprised us once, Sébasse and me, in the same sleeping bag. He was the one who wanted to, Ruth almost passed out when she saw us, and my grandfather put us in separate rooms after that. Separate rooms, Fernand likes that. The other room is right beside his, and after he's haunted mine, he can spill his seed a second time in the sheets of my sleeping friend, who wonders, when he wakes up, what that stain is on his pyjamas. With Sébastien I jump off the end of the dock, we hunt animals, we play at being adventurers, explorers, knights, the forest is enchanted and full of snakes, werewolves, and when he saves my life, I thank him by polishing his long hero's sword. With Sylvie we do the same things, except that she always calls time out to talk to me about her love for Sébastien, she wants to know if I think he loves her, if he talks to me about her, he held her hand the other day all through recess. Often we sit down to talk and she tries to make me feel bad for pushing her into the little ravine full of stinging hazel trees. After, I'm less tempted to mistreat her. In any case, it's a lot less interesting without Sébastien there to laugh or to come up with another crazy idea, a new outrage to inflict on her. I almost succeed in drowning her by accident once, pushing her off the dock, but without her cousin there, something is missing, I have no one to share my exploits with and to laugh at her distress. My grandfather Fernand thinks I'm going to marry Sylvie one day, because he also tortured Ruth when he was young, and now it's love. He's even going to give us the cottage where our first beautiful memories were made.

Sébastien and I do lots of things without my grand-parents knowing, we go down the slope towards the lake, passing through the ferns, to jump in in secret. On the dock, hidden by the trees, we take off all our clothes so as not to go back in all wet and tip my grandmother off that we've gone in swimming without any adults around. We dive, we dog-paddle, and then we go back to the dock to start all over again. I'm not on a hockey team like him and I'm surprised to see him so shameless, he has a penis too, between his legs, he shows it to me, it doesn't bother him. We try all sorts of things, Sébastien and I, we always put our hands where we shouldn't, in dark holes at the bottoms of trees, we taste everything we find, worms, insects. We build a camp in the woods, not far from the cottage, without telling anyone, we work at building it for a whole summer, dreaming of the things we'll be able to do once our cabin is finished. When we do finish it, we get bored. The planks are all laid, the door opens and closes, it locks, we've left holes for the windows, there are benches, room for two or three sleeping bags, and nothing more to build. The camp is complete, and there's nothing left for us to do.

THE LITTLE CEMENT WALL

Kevin comes back from the North after four hard months on the job. To please his son, to spend some time with him, towards the end of summer he takes him to the Saint-Félicien zoo. The little kid is happy as a clam, he'll be able to see real live lions, or at least what most resembles them that can be found there: the cougars. All along the secondary road that links Chicoutimi to Saint-Félicien, Croustine keeps asking how long it will be before they arrive. The road is long for the youngster, who has to stop and pee at Alma and then at Roberval because his father bought him a big brain-blue frozen Slushie at the corner store where he stopped for gas, and he drank it too fast. Between Roberval and Saint-Félicien, the boy sleeps. He dreams about the lions he will soon see closer up than he ever would have imagined.

After paying the entry fee, Kevin picks up a plan of the site. This way to the cougars. Croustine is impatient, he runs ahead of his father, tells him to hurry, he's afraid he'll miss them. It's early in the morning and the zoo is deserted, the woman at the gate assures them that this is the best time to see the animals outside their lairs, because it's not yet too hot. The cougars are in a kind of ditch and they look down on them from a balcony whose cement guardrail has glass panes you can see through. Croustine spends an eternity with his hands glued to the enclosure's windows, not saying a word, studying the animals' every move. He's insatiable, it's the first time he's seen real live animals—not counting the little bichon that he knew all too briefly. The cougars could be stuffed, they're so still, stretched out nonchalantly in the shadow of the firs, their natural habitat. None of them assumes the proud pose of Grandfather Lambert's lion. Finally Kevin gets impatient. Croustine, however, doesn't want to miss a thing, asks for five minutes more.

The zoo begins to fill up. A happy family are thrilled on seeing the cougars, and ask Kevin to take a picture of them. Kevin recognizes this stupid family that lives near the des Tourterelles traffic circle. He knows them, but neither the father nor the mother of Sébastien and Marie-Loup remember this man who went out very early and came back very late, and who was guilty of their niece's death a few years earlier. The Forciers position themselves in front of the little cement wall, and smile for the camera. Kevin wonders what on earth they're going to find worthwhile in this photo after they get home and see nothing but the enclosure's exterior. He tells himself that domestic happiness has to survive many bad snaphots, and with the pricey instrument in his hands, he thinks of making off with it just to introduce a bit of tragedy into this radiant family tableau. Sébastien's father, seeing the picture on the camera's screen, asks him to do it over: you can't see the youngest child. Kevin Lambert grits his teeth, he feels like dropping it on the ground, this digital camera full of silly souvenirs. They hoist the little girl onto the cement so she won't be cut out of the composition—intentionally awkward—of the photograph. Mounted on the low wall, she is almost as tall as her father, and that makes her laugh.

Croustine, who sees Marie-Loup on top of the wall, also wants to mount it, right away. Kevin agrees, on one condition: that they can then move on, there are other animals to see. Kevin takes his son in his arms, perches him on the guardrail, keeps his hand on the child's back as a protective gesture. Then an idea lights up his frontal lobe. A dumb idea he will regret. The sort of idea that occurs to a mind fatigued from lack of sleep, running solely on caffeine. One of those thoughts that should never be acted on. He will deeply regret what he's about to do, but that morning, at the Saint-Félicien zoo, a curse pronounced years earlier is going to hit its mark. Kevin Lambert, on this September morning when destinies converge, gently nudges his son in the back.

The boy loses his footing, falls onto the wall, one knee on the cement, then his body slumps forwards and his helpless hands have nothing to grip, what with the void gaping wide beneath him. He emits a high-pitched scream, then, in an instant, hits the ground hard, down in the enclosure. The merry mother starts to scream as the father freezes, she emits the same howl she'll bring forth on the night when her husband, in a fit of madness, with an inexplicable bubble in his brain after a remission of several years, will slit her throat and those of her two children, before turning the blade on himself. Grabbing at the telephone in his pocket, the father drops his five-thousand-dollar camera onto the cement. In the enclosure, the idle cougars are awakened by all the fuss, as they are by the solid piece of meat that is whimpering and trying to raise himself on his broken legs. A choice morsel for the cougars, who have not yet been fed that day. They eagerly tear their meal to shreds as it writhes beneath their fangs, so unlike the hunks of dead horsemeat on which they normally dine. The moment passes, and Croustine as well. The animals are soon sated. For appearances' sake they are put to sleep, and what's left of the little body is wrapped in a white sheet inside an ambulance.

FALLING APART

The murder of the child Croustine, perpetrated under tragic circumstances by Chicoutimi with its ill-starred spells, is but one in a long line. Like the other children, Croustine remains. In my masturbatory fantasies I sleep with his father the better to have him die, I lay my cards out on the table so he will pay for this death that has been passed on, carved into the earth of the chill cemetery where a child, alone, weeps among the toads. Croustine grew up only to die. I already feel, in reading the arcanum on the garden table, the fateful filiation that will complete itself, death borne along like an offering. I will follow it through the generations: thanks to Croustine, Kevin will die, then old man Lambert. The tarot says so. The death harvested among the yellow clover growing on the child's grave will be the first component of our apocalyptic trinity; Chicoutimi will pay for its slaughtered children, for the children dotting its cemetery, the little graves where we can count on our fingers the number of years bridging the dates carved in stone. Croustine's devouring on September 11, 2001, was met with almost total indifference. He had the bad luck to die on one of the rare days where in the history books there's no room to spare for unsung dramas, minor angels. They're forgotten.

All through his childhood he tries to recover from the silence shrouding his assassination, eclipsed by the dust from September 11's far-off fallen Towers. Kevin Lambert is set free, thanks to insufficient evidence. The police, on that day, are too busy entering houses where people have barricaded themselves in, waiting for the end of the world. On that catastrophic day, the day when Croustine and the Twin Towers are brought down, the inhabitants of Saguenay and Lac-Saint-Jean think they are witnessing Armageddon. Of course, these are imbeciles who know nothing of the apocalypse that is truly under way, of the last judgment being prepared, the dark measures being taken in suburban basements. In this hour of eternity's last calls, the people of Chicoutimi are the sightless workers paving the way for disasters yet to come. They have been groomed to be afraid, that's all the world has taught them: the fear and the dread of fear that gnaws away at their bones and rots them from within. They will die from it. They will die for not celebrating the beauty of an empire in its downfall, for shutting their eyes to the prophecies being broadcast twenty-four hours out of twenty-four, seven days out of seven, on their pathetic screens, for loathing what is sublime in the collapse, beyond the horizon, of the summit of our world's debris.

On September 11, 2001, I am in grade six, and I lament the fact that those planes did not bring down our school. I implore the heavens to send another, I want us to be crushed as well. They turned on the news right in our class, it's a historic moment, a declaration of war, it's important that we see it. But there is no war in the wake of the crashed airplane, in the shards of glass and broken tiles; the real war is growing apace in Chicoutimi households with every catastrophe, and is being set out by the side of the road on garbage day. In the Réjean-Tremblay School classroom, we hear the journalists describing the attacks moment by moment. Once again I sense that history has left us in the lurch. Once again it has gone elsewhere to mount its show. The beginning of the end is showing signs of life in strange, imagined worlds that are far away, on territory never yet glimpsed by the students in my class. But these are ersatz disasters, a prologue to the dead who will disembowel the land and wreak havoc in our time. You don't reduce to dust what is already dust, and if Chicoutimi is intact on this day, it's not because the apocalypse has forsworn us, but because it is we who will be at its epicentre.

On the local news we see crazed residents preparing themselves as best they can. They hope for an end, they invoke it with their silence. They empty the grocery stores, lay up provisions, shut the doors, block the windows.

A fallen Tower sanctions racist urges, whose roots in this land run deep: an Arab family is assaulted on the sidewalk. We need the Other to justify all those deaths, we do not see that the attack has come from within ourselves, from the heart of our civilization. Those who are civic-minded, responsible, thrill-seeking, ought to know: in the daycares of our local schools, powerful antibodies are putting forth shoots. In the Canadian school books that fill our Lavoie bags, words of havoc are being inscribed charting a course for our wild devisings: to bite down on the gun barrel and blow out our brains. A poison's antidote issues always from the poison itself. During the first days of my sixth year in elementary school, I already know that it is neither evil nor good that makes the earth tremble and drives fanatics to throw themselves onto the flames.

I hear the cries and alerts in the darkness of September 10, 2001. All that we're shown the next morning, on all the television channels, I've already seen. I have known it intimately, from the inside, I have borne it with me every night of my life and I will continue to harbour it beyond that fateful day, I will carry it with me forever, and when I lay it down at last, when I activate the detonator, Chicoutimi will be shaken to its foundations. My vision will cease to be once the explosions begin. Behind my closed lids, as it replicates itself each night, I see the Tower, a tarot card of my mother's that features a spire in flames.

When I was a child, Viviane forbade me to touch her occult game, which she slid over her damp hands each night to give herself some sense of what awaited her in life. She refused to lend me her cards, she knew what I would find, she had seen the snake wrap itself around my ankle and creep up my thigh, she saw the future of my future and she was afraid. This great tower, which in my dreams appears as the Twin Towers, melds with the image of Kevin Lambert's penis; I know that the Twin Towers are my member and his, that their shuddering was a masturbation, and that their explosion was a climax. I tell our futures, wreathed in New York's smoke. I cheat and help myself to my dead mother's tarot deck when my grandparents leave me alone in the house. At night when the card the Tower, the sixteenth in the tarot, first appears to me in a dream, I understand that the people shown there are not walking on their hands to amuse themselves, as my mother always told me, but are falling from a building in flames, assaulted by heavenly thunderbolts. It is not joy that I read on their faces, but agony at the haste with which the abyss is opening up before them, this void that gives them no succour, into which they are falling, hands first, like little Croustine into the cougars' enclosure. On the ground, their hands splinter. Death, again, has imposed itself. The body is meat, carved up and ingested. The papers, on September 12, show no interest in Croustine's story. It is relegated to a few short lines in a brief news item. And yet his death is no less real than that of the three thousand people onto whom the flaming Towers have collapsed. Croustine marks his third birthday shortly afterwards, and remains an accessory to his own destruction.

THE DRAMA OF HAPPY FAMILIES

The employees of the Saint-Félicien wild animal zoo respond in exemplary fashion to the accident that precipitated the child's death, so they contend in a meeting the following week, and so it is stated in the local paper's news report. Everyone at his or her post, calming the confused clientele, evacuating the site, contacting the emergency services, it all unfolds as if Croustine's demise was planned out long in advance. A guard at the zoo reacts swiftly, firing darts from her gun to put the aggressive beasts to sleep, but already Croustine's small carcass has been stripped of its flesh. They don't know quite what to do with Kevin Lambert, frozen to the spot and facing serious accusations from the happy family. Many will claim that the bloody scene, this gratuitous act, is what will trigger Sébastien's father, who some months later kills his son, his daughter, and their mother with a long knife right out of a horror film.

I am in grade six at the time of this family drama that has such a disastrous impact on Chicoutimi and the entire Des Oiseaux community. That Saturday morning, when all the houses on Rue des Tourterelles have the disquieting air of the day after a tragedy, a Purolator van comes to a stop. The delivery man walks through the traffic circle's newly plowed snow and passes very near to a huge mound left in the middle of the street. Soon he will climb the steps of 2013, will knock to ask for Sébastien, will hand him a package, will see the excitement in his eyes just before he runs off to the kitchen for a pair of scissors, eager to unwrap the skateboard he's been anticipating, ordered from an American site for his twelfth birthday. The delivery man will ask for a signature. Sébastien will look at his mother, who will quietly nod her head, smiling to see her son so happy that it is his own signature that is being requested. He will do what adults do when they are asked for such a thing: make a sort of illegible scrawl of which he will be proud. But this Saturday morning no one answers at 2013. The delivery man is there waiting to see if there is some light moving at the end of the hallway. Nothing. Not a breath, nothing stirring in the deserted house. He sticks a piece of paper to the door saying that there is a package to be picked up at the drugstore post office. Before leaving, he might have taken a closer look through the diamond in the frosted window: he would have seen, on the hallway's white walls, traces of blood left by a hand that must have been leaning there. He would have been able to alert the police, who would have broken down the door. But just as the delivery man is about to peer in, a rumbling is heard at the end of the street: the snow blower come to dispense with the mountain of snow in the middle of the traffic circle.

Chicoutimi, unable to bear the news of two trage-
dies on the same street, even several years apart, tries to
delay the disclosure of the second. But the story sells well,
there is perhaps collusion between the local papers, people
wonder if the street is under a curse. The dark business of
Sébastien's family makes the front page the day after the
dead bodies are discovered. That is how Madeleine, the
children's grandmother, learns about it. She sets fire to
the paper and curses her son with a deep and agonizing
howl. She has always saved the press clippings whenever
they talked about her grandson's hockey team winning
a tournament, or her granddaughter excelling in a regional
gymnastic competition. She's stored them proudly in a ring
binder when they've written about her son, a good man,
adored by the entire town, holding a plasticized cheque
given to a food bank or donated to cancer research. She's
kept the articles outlining his involvement in municipal
politics, and even the advertisements from when he was
a real estate agent. But she does not save the front page
with the photograph of the ambulance in front of 2013
Rue de Tourterelles, that front page with its macabre news
spelled out in big red letters. She does not save the arti-
cle describing the triple murder committed by her son,
she keeps no page from any paper making mention of his
monstrous suicide.

PUTTING TO DEATH

I scan the skies for the best way to damn you, Chicoutimi, I want to know you utterly, to master every facet of this landscape I despise. I yearn to see you laid waste. I long to witness your death throes, to see your helpless eyes begging for mercy. But I know no mercy. I can no longer await your destruction, longing for a catastrophe that will end your days and wipe you from the map. No, it is I who will destroy you, Chicoutimi. Seeking counsel from the sky, talking to the stars and the occult powers, to all the dead you harbour within you, I have found my calling. I have dreamed each night of your end. Your destruction will be my doing, my pyrotechnics will be stunning; only saints and hypocrites will balk at the scrupulous annihilation I am plotting. You will die with the children's chaste laughter in your ears, and this ruination will stun the entire world. You are the abscess festering in the void, the tumour gnawing away at nothingness, Chicoutimi, and when deliverance will come, all will cheer your disappearance. The world will be burdened with you no more, will no longer see the world through your lens, in the light of your vistas, your buried depths. You will take your place at last in the dustbin of history, will only survive in some awkward, overlong sentence in an omitted paragraph or perhaps one deleted in editing, or at the bottom of a page in a silly footnote citing another out-of-print work, impossible to find. The accounts will retain only your name, a tiny dot on ancient maps of the world and of the heavens, those *mappa mundi* that future children will scan, dreaming as one dreams while gazing on monsters that once populated mysterious seas. No one can hold in memory what is no more, no one can remember for him who forgets, no one can harbour a memory as it slips away, no one can bear witness for you, Chicoutimi.

After their death it is Madeleine, Sébastien's paternal grandmother, who takes care of him and his sister. Sébastien's father grew up in the house where the two murdered children go to live. No one, except Madeleine, attends his burial. Her face is awash with tears of loathing and shame. She leaves Marie-Loup with her brother, no question of bringing her there. The mad killer is interred without ceremony on the first day of spring. The funerals for the mother and children take place a week later, the Chicoutimi cemetery is filled with people under a rain melting the last of the snow and waking, quietly, the frozen toads near the graves of Sébastien, Marie-Loup, and their mother. Sébastien in his grave is beautiful. He's been combed and well dressed, he looks like a Greek statue, one of those that immortalize the beauty of the boy soldiers who launched stones and battled giants. Marie-Loup has roses and flower buds in her hair. Delicate flowers that you murder in cutting their stems are blooming, like the living dead, in the eschatological hair of the little girl. The mother's coffin is closed: you do not display the faces of the disfigured dead. The end of the world comes to Chicoutimi one more time on that day. Sylvie, dead and buried, fittingly honours the death of my friend, shedding tears before his candlelit body, exposed, the body for which she burns with desire, just like me, just like every student at Réjean-Tremblay School.

Sylvie, Sébastien, my two friends from elementary school, dead before we entered high school, join my mother and my grandparents in limbo. Like all things beautiful and true, which we honour and in which we believe, whose beauty and authenticity we celebrate, you will die, Chicoutimi. All beautiful things self-destruct in the end. You will have been there to give me life, and I will have survived to put you to death. You will not go quietly, Chicoutimi. But your sullied earth will become fertile once more thanks to the blood spilled, and we will all applaud when the malevolent crows come to drink up the last of your blood, phlegm, and bile.

PART
THREE

THE DEATH OF OTHERS

Of course, I too am already dead. The grave that yawned and into which I was lowered was well dug, measured out to the last millimetre, and old deformed toads are now leaping obstinately up against my stone, maddened by the pesticides strewn over the green grass. I am the corpse, the child killed by Grandfather Fernand at the age of four, almost five, one autumn night, a last weekend at the cottage before winter, he was enraged and smothered me, I bit hard and he struck me, I had his blood in my mouth along with his sperm, couldn't spit it out under the pillow where I was dying, his old arms had lost none of their strength. They found me in the lake. I had never paid any heed to the warnings not to go swimming alone, and so the accident was all too plausible. This was well before the beginning of the story I've been telling. I died a child before starting school, Viviane and Ruth mourned me for a while, I came back to console them. I was perhaps the first child to return; a Chicoutimi plot to preserve the reputation of a prominent man, the former school principal whose thick office door muffled all the cries of guilty boys. What would Chicoutimi not do to protect an honourable white man, the architect of its destructive machines, of its sorrowful buildings, how far would my native city go to uphold its infamous saintliness? Far enough to bring back dead children. To cleanse them of the signs of their own homicide, to force them to live a bit longer. I am the body sliced up and dispersed by a snow blower one winter morning, the one carved into by a sordid blade, I am the shock that did in the teetering boy with the sharpened lead of a pencil, I am the teeth that tore into the body, the beast that roared and drank blood. I am those deaths and all the others. Over and over, I died struck by a car speeding through the midnight darkness. But like the other children, I remain. It is not death that would have me leave Chicoutimi. They buried me and I entered more fully into its depths, merged with them, I am its fetid water, the poison that circulates and benumbs its vital functions. Bombs are about to explode.

IN THE SUBURB OF NOTHINGNESS

The Chicoutimi of my high school days was no more than a mid-sized town. Some countryside too, with the fields at Laterrière that you sometimes passed on the way to the park and then down to Quebec City. I couldn't see that far from the school roof where I liked to install myself. Below, people saw the soles of my new Converses that I'd bought at Amnesia in Place du Royaume, and they shouted: come down, Faldistoire, it's dangerous, if you don't come down, you're going to be in trouble, how did you get up there? There was a nice view from the top of the school, I saw the neighbourhood streets all around, I saw Boulevard Talbot, the part on top of the hill. I saw far, but not as far as the lost motel just before the highway, the motel that made you wonder who slept there: the truckers and their boy hookers who left by taxi in the morning. The warehouses here, there, and everywhere, a barren zone and a golf course and fields: I didn't see them either. My feet hung down as I sat at the corner of the school, a dangerous perch, I liked making myself dizzy up above the empty parking lot as I observed Chicoutimi, a nothing suburb, a suburb of nothingness. A suburb surrounding a common grave where they put the dead bodies, a huge black hole, a lost vortex leading to another dimension, also lost—a shortcut to nowhere, a door to hell over which my running shoes gaily dangled. Chicoutimi beneath my feet, crying to me to come back down, and threatening me with a variety of consequences. But the weather was good and the view was fine, the vista was all bathed in light, my kingdom, the vast land lit by the day's late rays that went to die behind the Valin hills. I asked myself what would remain of Chicoutimi if it were to crash down on us, that huge ball of fire. I looked at the colours being born in the sky, the reds and the oranges tinting the clouds, I traced out the town's silhouette, I followed the brightness as it glided across the roofs of houses, of the university buildings, I imagined them all destroyed. Soon they would be no more. It was written, I knew, I had read it in my dreams, I had read it in the shapes of clouds over the Rivière-du-Moulin park, in the furrows formed by the neighbourhood bungalows, in the films chosen to rent at the video store where I worked, in the tarot cards I'd learned to interpret with Sylvie's mother on a big apple-wood table. I'd heard it softly murmured in the voices commanding me to come down. The Indian summer was warm, the light was pure, and already I saw the latent flames on the rims of the houses. The dead in the cemetery reminded me of it every night when, during my slumber, I went back to sleep in my grave: I was going to destroy Chicoutimi. Perhaps a project too vast for the child I still was, dogged by the caretakers trying to scale the steep ladder. I had to use my body as a missile, to let myself drop onto the cluster of teachers shouting themselves hoarse beneath my feet, imploring me to conduct them to their final end, towards the ravenous hole lying in wait for them in the cemetery, close to the toads.

LIFE COMES FIRST

I started high school one September day at Lycée de Chicoutimi, a private school whose tuition my father paid out of my inheritance. He'd talked to me often about this school right in the heart of the Murdock neighbourhood, of its large schoolyard and its wood, of the river and the big waterfall into which a student fell during his time there. Of the cemetery in the back where we entertained ourselves shifting the priests' gravestones around to change the identities of the long-dead teachers. All through high school I lived at my father's. We'd tracked him down a little while after my grandmother Ruth's death and the suicide of my grandfather Fernand, and after the mother of my dead friend Sylvie had temporarily adopted me. At the end of grade six, almost everyone in my group went to the public high school, and I wanted to go too, but my father chose to send me to the private school, and I had no say in the matter. At least Sylvie and Sébastien followed me to the Lycée. I never understood why you had to pay to go to this school where all the teachers were mental and the students totally disturbed. In the first year, two students could not adjust to the transition from elementary to high school, and killed themselves. At Christmastime, we were the grade with the smallest number of suicides, and we received a beautiful banner, *LIFE COMES FIRST*, that we hung up in the lounge. It's often been said that death is contagious and that it circulates like the plague; our chemistry teacher was found in his office after the holidays, his brains splattered onto his leather chair, and the enamel at the tips of his teeth shattered from having been clamped down on the gun barrel too tightly. We honoured him, but it wasn't a great loss: however much I pretended, I couldn't believe in the "value" of this loathsome man's life, and I secretly celebrated each new death of a member of his species as one more step towards the elimination of the male sex. Every suicide caused a little fuss around the school, which multiplied its preventive meetings with their empty arguments designed to sell us on the importance of living. I had to see the psychologist once a week, I wasn't out of the woods after elementary school, they were intent on protecting me from myself, given the yen for things suicidal I inherited from my mother and grandfather. Actually, I would have liked them to let me croak in peace if I wanted to. The psychologist made sure I wouldn't catch a case of death during our long sessions, which had the advantage of enabling me to skip the dumbest and most boring classes given by the assortment of loonies, madmen, and ex-cons hired by the Lycée de Chicoutimi with the idea of *forming a responsible leader to excel in the community.*

For five years the Lycée continued to bleed my grand-parents' legacy dry, the Lycée that had always been a drain on the savings of Chicoutimi families, having them believe in the importance of *lending an ear to the young person in order to partner with him in the discovery of his talents and to help him to fully flourish in an environment where he will take satisfaction in the progress he makes in a spirit of co-operation and excellence.* The Lycée charged money for the admissions test, each year's registration, the uniform that had to be changed every two years because we grew too fast, the shorts and T-shirts for physical education because of the new logo, every extracurricular activity and the materials required for it. The Lycée, a business masquerading as a school, with all the good intentions—bogus—of the teachers who, only once a year, on the day for parental visits, made as if they gave a damn.

I became Victor's friend on orientation day, which we spent doing nothing, just sitting in the lounge. I didn't understand why I was there listening to an unctuous principal strutting about and talking to us about the colour of the report cards and the envelopes we had to have signed by our parents, the oranges we had to sell to finance our beautiful school. In comparison, elementary school seemed much more demanding and relevant. Victor commented on all the teachers filing by. It was the first day, but he knew them already, he knew what he was getting into: the fifth child in a family of six, he had four brothers and sisters who had attended the Lycée de Chicoutimi. One of his sisters had killed herself the previous year, because she was being badly harassed by a kind of punk, Victor was going to show me who he was so we could hate him. While we were being introduced to those who would be our teachers for five years—they seemed as pleasant as an open wound—he talked to me at length about our new school, shared with me all the information his brothers and sisters had passed on to him. Entering the Lycée, we already despised certain teachers, as well as knowing the secret lives of some others, including the principal, still blabbing away at the centre of the room (about how, I think, you were not supposed to spit on the walls). The past year he had left his wife, who was gravely ill in her bones, for a former Lycée student, just newly adult and now studying at CEGEP.

SPELLS

The day after my grandparents were buried, I was forced to go and live at Sylvie's, no longer having Fernand or Ruth to take care of me and to make me macaroni with sausages. So I became important to her mother, who showered me with attention, love, and strange ointments during the long rituals to which I was submitted in the shed behind 2008 Rue des Tourterelles. Sylvie's mother was a witch who thought magic could have a positive influence on my fate. She said that many people were dying around me: I had to be purified. Covering me with talismans, she tied me to a kitchen chair and cut my hair, hurt me with the tight ropes that kept me from moving, gave me a little jar in which there floated the yellow eye of a little cat. Sylvie's mother grasped hold of me, licked at my body with her oregano breath, pricked the tip of my finger so a drop of blood would fall into some dark oil that she used to inscribe me with alchemical symbols. Every night for almost a month the sorceress swooned over me, her long hair reeking of perfume. Sometimes she pointed gnarled sticks at the sky, spouting formulas and invoking angels or demons, her eyes rolled back in her head. My eyes burned because of the incense and the odours from the fish entrails, onion, and garlic that she strewed all around. During long nights when tarots burned and metals melted onto my skin, all those I had lost and who were entombed beneath the green toads in the Chicoutimi cemetery filed by me as if by enchantment. I saw again Viviane, Fernand, Ruth, Sylvie, and Sébastien.

Sylvie's mother was arrested while I was at school. Found in her shed were dead cats that had vanished from nearby homes, dead dogs people thought had fled, wild and domestic birds, and various remains that all had one thing in common: eyes extracted at the point of a dagger, to furnish an essential ingredient for the complex preparation of her ointments. When the affair came to light, I was questioned by the police, but I didn't want to talk to them. I told them anything at all, I contradicted myself on purpose with each sentence, and when they insisted that I wasn't making sense, I spat in their faces because of my oppositional defiant disorder the investigators knew by heart from their DSM-IV. They tracked down my real biological father, the school psychologist warned them to keep me well away from the animal killer and said they should send me off to my begetter. The psychologist explained to the judge, assuming his pseudo-erudite, sorry-to-have-to-say-it air, that I was mad. Meanwhile his face was flushed with bilious professional pride, his exultant mug over which, during his entire speech, I wanted to pass a cheese grater. The witch was condemned to a few days of incarceration plus a healthy fine, she was cured of her murderous impulses by locking her into a Chicoutimi prison cell where real psychopaths were languishing, head cases who behaved incoherently and others, patient as silkworms, waiting to resume their employment at the Lycée. She came out a few days later, then went back to live in her Des Oiseaux bungalow. Her clientele, after this morbid discovery, doubled. Her cruelty was perceived, by the inhabitants of Chicoutimi, as irrefutable proof of her divinatory gift.

LET US ABORT

Sex in the Lycée was neither easy nor free, it involved a complex system of transactions, reproducing in miniature Chicoutimi's social classes, but substituting subtle notions of popularity for the concept of financial status; my friends and I were the most average students in the most average category. Sébastien entered the Lycée, once he was dead, through the front door. To the compassionate consideration he received thanks to his brutal murder was added the students' admiration for his small rebellions against authority. On orientation day, young people from other schools were whispering his name. We were reading "Sébastien Forcier, that's him," on their lips, they were talking about how game he was, how he didn't give a damn about power and put the teachers in their place when they stepped out of line. We all wanted to have him in our class, we all wanted him to lead us down near the falls, behind the Lycée, at noon, for us to take off our clothes and for him to do with us whatever he liked.

And yet as of our first year I was no longer his friend. Our groups formed and unformed to stabilize in our final year, and he ceased to be part of mine. In the hallways and in class we continued to exchange polite "yo's," to show that we remembered the secrets sealed in our memories. All through high school he laughed at my jokes as I did at his, but we no longer dared to make room for that complicity which had bound us so powerfully. I explained to Victor that, in any case, I no longer recognized him since the funerals. And in any case he hated gays and everything that came with them, he beat up the little red-headed faggot during recess, and I was afraid he'd do the same thing to me if he learned that his friends on the football team all lined up to be sucked off in the empty science department at noon. I distanced myself a little from Sylvie as well, even if we maintained our special bond, unbreakable despite her ghostliness. We didn't really spend time together, but I was always there for her, when she was dumped by her boyfriends or given a hard time by the popular girls. I went with her when, in third year, she had an abortion. It was at a beautiful, clean clinic, she'd made an appointment, and they'd told her that the operation was painless. The selection of magazines in the waiting room was good, they were all recent, and there were at least five or six different kinds. We waited in silence for her to be called by the nurse. Sylvie was calm, she murmured in my ear that the girl in front of us was crying because she was thinking about all the wonderful things her future offspring might have done with his life. I was left alone with her when Sylvie was called into the doctor's office, and soon it was Viviane I was seeing there in front of me, waiting to have excised the ulcer that I had been. I'd have liked it if she had aborted me. I saw myself as a little fetus extracted from my mother's body, and the vision moved me. I would have preferred never to have existed, never to know Chicoutimi and its disasters. Oh to die at birth like Victor's cousin, a little rascal who wrapped his cord five or six times around his neck. My mother could have dropped me to the ground when I was very young, forgotten me in the car, or put me in the microwave, as so many parents do with their unwanted offspring. I blamed Viviane for having rammed my childhood down my throat. I loved the scenarios in which my mother gave me life just in order to take it from me, just as I inspired desire in Kevin with the tip of a finger or my tongue on his member only to immediately refuse him, shut myself in and masturbate to cheap porn, jacking myself off to sleep, my head in the books fallen from the shelf, while he finally gave up trying to make me open the door. My own abortion moved me, I wondered whether it was not the noblest act of all, the loftiest Viviane could have performed, the ultimate triumph over nature's barbarism, over the childhood that attacks you from within like a parasite, whether it should have been my mother's obligation towards the entire human race. Sylvie came out of the room a few minutes later, holding her little tumour in a brown paper bag. We fed it to the cats. I was jealous of her reject.

ALMANACH

We were doing our math problems when the teacher brought him in, he'd changed schools, we didn't know why, there was just his name: Almanach. We laughed our heads off when, in front of everybody, the teacher asked him to repeat it and he had to say again: my name is Almanach. We liked our class, things were going fine without him, we knew everybody, even the two or three new ones, we'd already decided whether we hated them or if they were cool enough for us to invite to parties. We'd already seen him, we vaguely remembered him, he was popular in elementary school, but high school was something else. Within thirty seconds he was toast: his strange name, his dark skin, his crooked teeth, his black frizzy hair, he must have come from another country, he talked like a Frenchman, he seemed really straight with his shirt tucked into his pants. We all hoped that the teacher wouldn't come and put his desk beside ours, that we wouldn't have to study alongside him. The bell rang, we all rushed to get dressed and go out and bum some cigarettes from our friends before the buses arrived: it seemed he was so sharp that he'd skipped a year, that he'd killed someone at Félix-Antoine-Savard, that his mother was rich and she'd changed his school when the teachers gave him a hard time, that he spoke Arabic, that his father was a terrorist who'd hidden out in Quebec to stir things up. The year passed, our rumours made the rounds, we laughed in his face coming back from our week off, we forgot him over the summer.

Start of the fourth year: we all said we hoped we wouldn't be in the same group as him. We were secretly happy when we saw that he was in our class, it meant we were safe: we wouldn't be hassled too much, there would always be someone worse off than we were. He was a bit ghostly, roamed the hallways and never came into the common room. Braces were slowly fixing his teeth, and Almanach left us alone: he stopped trying to be cool, to want to impress us and be part of the gang. We still didn't go so far as to talk to him, but we picked on others, we got drunk on Coors Light, and we crouched down when the music went low, low, low, low; we frenched each other fast before our parents came to get us, they were there at midnight on the dot, we used Axe before getting into the car so as not to smell of pot when our mothers came too near.

We kept busy, we forgot him. It all came back to us when we ran into him in the showers. The faggy sports he did gave him disturbing abs, he had hair on his chest, his pubic hair was as dark as that on his head, which was six feet in the air. We started to hate him again, tried to tell stories about him in the usual don't-give-a-shit way you do, then one day an unexpected twist in the plot, a detour in the scenario. It was raining, the soccer game was cancelled, we went running in the gym even if we didn't have to, there we were just the two of us in the locker room, just the two of us face to face in the shower. For the first time we talked a bit, looked each other in the eyes, frenched for a long time, sodomized awkwardly on the bench. He came with his solid cock, his wide shoulders, my hand thrust into his thick head of hair, we held each other tight, our skin flushed, we skipped the afternoon.

ABSENCES

The absentee notes and those for unjustified lateness add up quickly when, in the class, you're not yet seated when the bell rings and a teacher, a bit full of himself, a bit of an asshole it goes without saying, decides to clamp down: you have to be strict because if you give them an inch, they'll take a mile. Monsieur Certeau checked, in every class, to see if we were wearing the right shoes; the dress code forbade sneakers at the Lycée de Chicoutimi, this was a sign and signature of a quality educational institution. When I forgot to take them off coming back at noon, if they were dirty or I was wearing no shirt over my T-shirt, Certeau sent me out into the hallway to get a note. That was our favourite time in the class, we did what we wanted in the hallways, we spied on other classes, we made funny faces at the windows, we passed by the science wagon at the door to the laboratory and stole a frog, a cow's heart, something that was going to be dissected, and we stuck it into Certeau's pigeonhole.

The teachers at the Lycée loved to tell us about their lives, as if we cared. Seeing them carrying on in front of a bunch of idiot students, bug-eyed with their stories that had no beginning or end, that were of no interest whatsoever, those lame slices of life, with nothing about them that would give them a bit of bite, those little personal experiences, predigested, prerehearsed, recounted identically in every class, with the joke in the same place, seeing them flatter their own half-wit egos trying to get a laugh out of us, a tear of admiration, I was sorry that their mothers hadn't done what Sylvie did when, in a moment of insight, she got rid of her embryo. Despite everything, I valued Monsieur Certeau, who entertained me with his ramblings; we soon decided that he actually believed in the idiocies he reeled off. One day he told us, in a class on deforestation, that he'd once gone to the Amazon and had seen a snake at least this big swimming beside him in the river, he was with a guide that you hired there to take you into the jungle, they almost got lost and night in the Amazon was full of dangers in the densest forest in the world, with places the sun never reached, and where there were man-eating panthers and other creatures not yet even discovered. And men, too, who ate travellers, using their tibias as forks, who made big necklaces with their teeth, and burned their scalps to call up pagan powers. The guide had a long machete that scared him at first, he was at his mercy, he ate parrot, he showed us a photo with his guide in front of a huge mountain, a volcano he'd climbed, a desert he'd crossed, but we knew it was simple to Photoshop. We dismissed out loud all these imaginings, we amused ourselves finding our own truths in the midst of all the bullshit he was serving up by the shovelful, we knew very well for what kind of machete he'd hired the guide, he must have taken it right in the behind at night, in their tent, and with his cries awakened every poacher trying to snuff out threatened species in peace.

With Alex, Victor, Félicie, Almanach, we liked to invent lives for our teachers. They became comic characters in absurd and sadistic scenarios, we laughed loudly at the back of the class, we disturbed everyone, we got sent out for lack of respect, and we got another note for unjustified absence. Victor spiced up our stories with outrageous details. Alex had a gift for drawing and turned our teachers into caricatures that were handed around under our desks to everyone in the class. Monsieur Dostie as a math teacher who was bald and impetuous, with a vein that showed up on his temple whenever he got mad, his big voice that rattled our desks when he turned up the volume and froze everyone in the room, concealing his sadism and hoarding cadavers in his garage, raping some of them, his member as veined and shiny as his skull. Madame Conchita, with her elongated breasts, could do all sorts of stunts, they'd found her in a circus, in the monkey pen, that was why she had a moustache and conspicuous whiskers, that was why she spoke Spanish. The religion teacher smelled like the fish drawing in our catechism book, he still lived with his mother and took his bath with her, he was a virgin and masturbated while thinking of the Holy Spirit and all those stupidities, he'd wanted to be a priest but had been expelled for something involving a sacrament and an altar boy. Madame Marjolaine was our favourite teacher. We groped ourselves under our desks during the science lessons in which animal reproduction was the stimulant for many parallel fantasies. We were sure that she was the queen of sexuality, we imagined that she knew everything about blow jobs, anal penetration, cunts and cunnilingus, all those things we knew the names of but didn't know what they really were, and in time we would go and check out Google and watch a video that would give us our education, the real one.

WHAT THE TAROT SAID

I learned tarot from Sylvie's mother. In the garden behind my father's house I dealt the cards and arranged them, then sat at the table and predicted what was going to happen in Chicoutimi. I was bored with my life, and it was my trances that taught me the three things that might set me free from its storyline: clairvoyance, terrorism, and suicide. The future was there, on the tabletop, in those small paper rectangles that the fortune teller had one day shown me how to read in order to better understand the future, to foresee what was to come, and to cast the spell I needed to cast. Set down here are the insights recorded in gel crayon in my Canada notebooks, so that they might inspire others who hope to destroy our world. You must take these words as incantations:

XII—THE HANGED MAN. Your days are numbered. Sooner than you think, you will disappear. You will be beautiful, Chicoutimi. Everywhere we will see your remains, your lifeless streets, houses, schools, you will be ravaged like those cities caught up in nuclear disasters.

VIII—JUSTICE. I was taught to see the world through your eyes, Chicoutimi. I do not thank you for it. We must obliterate that greatness of soul, that whiff of nobility death imposes in its blindness, transmuting everything into something you label *virtue*. The child does not know how to name and does not believe in virtue. The child generates language and the word: a small bomb to explode what your honours claim to be. He owes you nothing, he must slay those who are to blame for his seeing the light of day. You are both father and mother, Chicoutimi, and to forge a new lineage I will demolish you.

XX—THE JUDGMENT. The time has come for auguries to come true, the time has come for fresh curses, I mean to say ancient prophecies really and truly fulfilled, those whose sources are more remote than our beginnings. At long last the sorcerers forced to hide themselves away will prevail. The day of card readers, tarot readers, spell casters, dervishes, shamans, necromancers, voodoo priestesses, magi, chiromancers, will arrive, their truth will be the only one still to prevail, defying once more a world betrayed, dishonoured, violated by all the realists and the virtuous, secretly assailed by all the proponents of good sense. We are not accountants, Chicoutimi.

XIII—ARCANUM WITH NO NAME. I see, looking down on this card with no name, that my own was written on yellow cardboard, in a grade two classroom, *FALDISTOIRE*.

XVI—THE TOWER. Behind this desk, in this school, we find him sitting, a felt pen in his hand. He will lose his family and his friends, will change houses a thousand times, will be forced to learn to live with ghosts, among ghosts. He will lay bare the occult powers of the penis and of hate, he will find in voluptuousness a splendid, tragic revenge, he will embrace a terrible, vital desire. Nothing is more glorious than a bomb or an orgasm, nothing is more powerful than their combined destructive action. He is in the art class drawing what he thinks is his home, but it is his grave that appears before him. His felt pens rub away at the paper, I see him and I enter into him a little, into Class 2B and his lesson in art, the papers passed under the table and the pencil sharpener offensives, the Nintendo cassettes hidden in his overalls pocket, the piano pushed into a corner, the cover closed, awaiting the music class.

XV—THE DEVIL. You must enter the classroom and kill the child again, you must kill Faldistoire so that from there on in, what remains will come undone.

VIVIANE'S FURNITURE

My father bought my grandparents' house after their death, a lovely dwelling, not too expensive, that no one wanted in any case because of the ghost stories circulating in the neighbourhood. He had it all refurnished, and I kept my room in the basement, where I did as I liked. All through high school I felt that at Rivière-du-Moulin I was at the other end of the world, and I complained loudly that my friends were far away and that I had to change buses at the terminal to get to school. I knew that Viviane would have flipped her lid because that was where all of Chicoutimi's drug addicts and murderers hung out, everyone knew, that's where they collared and recruited new members to set fire to houses in Domaine-du-Roy or to sell dope in the parks at noon when the daycare kids came out to play. When my father moved into our house, I decided to drag out all the old stuff that my mother had stored in the shed. I arranged the basement living room to make it identical to our old one in Des Oiseaux: I put the couches in the same place, the TV too, and even Viviane's ugly figurines on the furniture, in the exact same positions. Before putting everything in boxes, I'd photographed each piece, each chest of drawers with what there was on top, immortalizing her decorative creations with my Minolta. I found, at the back of the workroom, the awful canvases she'd insisted on painting, and I hung them in the stairway. My favourite was a portrait of me at the beach, when I was seven or eight, based on a picture my grandfather had taken during a trip to New Brunswick. It was impossible to tell, looking at it, that it was me in the picture, or even to be sure if it was a human being or a beach scene; Viviane's depiction of the world was closely aligned with her instinctive notions of abstraction.

I went back, one day, to near my mother's house. There were strangers living there now, and I hated them at first sight, so I returned with some friends in a car to trash their house and harass their children. Along with Victor, we parked and walked around the streets where I'd grown up. It was a beautiful autumn day. It was the Monday of a long weekend, and we were in second or third year. I was drawn to the footbridge where I'd been terrorized when I was younger because of the older druggie mad-dog skateboard kids who hung around there. I knew that it was the most direct way to Rue des Tourterelles. I found it still populated by teenagers like those out of my childhood. I was bigger, older, stronger than them now, and I wanted to make them pay for all they'd done to me. Victor and I decided to give them a scare; he always had a blade up his sleeve, like the guys with their hair combed back in James

Dean movies. The gamest kid in the gang came towards us, his friends trailing behind. He was beautiful. Victor threatened him with his blade, I led him under the cedars and made him let me suck him off, he came in my mouth, he cried from liking it, we left him there as we made off with what was left of his pride. He'd never say anything, he'd be too ashamed, the next day or that night, to tell the story. Our modus operandi was perfect.

Rue des Tourterelles was still drenched in the memory of the dramas that had taken place there. There was Sylvie, blown away by Kevin Lambert. There was Sébastien and all his family, murdered in cold blood by a ghastly father. Since the beginning of high school, I had not seen the clairvoyant of Des Oiseaux. She opened her door as if she knew I was about to ring, and ushered me inside. Her black hair had gone grey in spots, and when she talked, two or three hoarse voices exited her mouth simultaneously. She smiled at me. She seemed radioactive in her grey, dusty kitchen, and invited me to follow her out the back door. In the toxic air of chlorinated swimming pools, during this odd afternoon on the fortune teller's patio, I was tendered an object that I'd thought was lost forever. Sparing of words, her throat filled with gravel, the witch declined to tell me how she'd found it, how she'd been able to retrieve this notebook dropped into my mother's grave on the day she was buried. Seated in front of her tarot cards, she gave me back my grade two art class notebook in the pages of which everything, even then, had been foreseen. Just as I was about to hasten the final end, Chicoutimi's last gasp, just as I was preparing to fulfill the prophecy that had been entrusted to me, I was again reading her felt pen hieroglyphs. It was she who commanded me to act, and it was my firm intention to obey.

MY TRIPLE LOVES

Our story was essentially carnal. Kevin Lambert was on the good side of our Rivière-du-Moulin house, the right side as it happens; on the left were two broken-down old ladies who did nothing but complain about the noise from the lawn mower that my father made me push on summer Saturdays. I went one day to ring at Kevin's door to offer my services. I had to make some pocket money, my father couldn't always pay all my expenses, for the firecrackers and the bootleg bottles, the PJ Harvey and Guns N' Roses records, the video store films, the books by Jean Genet and Hannibal Lecter on which I spent my money. I babysat Kevin's kid over the summer between my third and fourth years of high school.

I had fun with Croustine. I taught him all sorts of things beyond his age: I showed him how to swear properly, I taught him to say it's *dess*, it's *begueuk*, it's *hard-core*, it's *vedge*, I had him listen to music groups, showed him how to deliver kicks to the balls when he was fed up, I tamed him, the little fucker, when he gave me a hard time, not wanting to take his bath, begging to watch TV with me past nine o'clock, his bedtime was eight o'clock, I knew it and so did he. When he finally fell asleep, I went into his father's bedroom without making any noise, on my guard so as not to be taken unawares. I rummaged in the drawers to feed my fantasies: underwear, an advice book on sex, massage oil. I masturbated with Kevin's lubricant while pretending that he was right behind me, that his hands were holding tight to my hips so he could enter me and assume control. I fantasized his thick, blond forearms, his muscled chest, and his depraved gaze while looking over my shoulder, I wore condoms, pretending my cock was his. Acting out the furious thrusts of his member made me ejaculate into his boxer shorts, which bore the salty odour from between his legs. I balled them up and put them back into the bottom of the laundry bin.

Kevin Lambert, the source of my most powerful fantasies, was twice my age, with a few white hairs showing through the blond, arms solid enough to strangle you, no known attraction to boys, it was an impossible love, one-way, I would die without having tasted of it. Then one night he came home early. He entered the house quietly and found me in his bedroom, twisted into his sheets, about to come. I jumped, I tried to hide. He got undressed and lay on top of me, grabbed me by the wrists, and thrust in his shaft without a word. As he was entering me, I was the first-born among the dead under his moist body, I was swooning and adjusting myself the better to receive him, to take him into me, to fill me with his warmth while I tore the skin off his back with my evil nails. Dream and reality fused in this sacred moment, the scene where I found myself soon started to mesh with what I'd been imagining a few minutes earlier, in thrall to my most ardent desires.

Almanach was jealous of my relationship with Kevin. It angered him, it wounded him, he talked to me about it in religion class, though I didn't listen, choosing to concentrate on our crazy old teacher telling us the story of his wretched life, his mean tricks, as he called them, the banalities he portrayed as serious crimes. There were no top-notch criminals in Chicoutimi, Almanach and I told ourselves that often. There were lots of little crooks, but no sublime thief, no glorious pyromaniac would ever emerge from the Lycée's schoolrooms, or infect the teaching body. They were backward adolescents hired to teach future backward adolescents and pass on their backward adolescent thinking, so as to ensure that Chicoutimi would remain the capital of pain it had been since its inception. Today's class was all about the Father, the Son, the Holy Ghost. The longer it went on, the more I hated the teacher and his Catholic mindset. My father said that within two years there would be no more religion taught in the schools, and that would be just fine. He wanted to sign me up for morals. But all my friends were in religion: I didn't feel like spending two periods a week in another class, along with the rejects. In catechism I sat beside Almanach and his dark, thick hair, where my fingers intruded while he shunned me, talked to me about Kevin, his blondness, his milky skin, his green eyes that softened his predatory animal's face, about my body beneath his in a state of ecstasy when we screwed on top of the stuffed animals in his basement. During all of fourth year another Trinity was constituted consisting of the three of us, Almanach, Kevin, and me, Faldistoire. I needed the two of them to be satisfied, I was in a way their holy ghost.

Kevin worked in the North, in the improvised kitchens of mines or work sites, I was afraid he would leave and never come back, I hated him for being indifferent to me, for never writing me, I wished he'd be involved in a tragic plane crash and die, it would be a beautiful ending to our story, a last organ chord, no place for little dramas, petty pains. I placed the tarot cards on the table, I recited an incantation, I pronounced a curse. I wanted an accident. A catastrophe. An airplane down on the peak of a northern mountain. He would survive the crash and would be forced to feed on human flesh. But the intense cold would kill him a few minutes before help arrived. They would discover his body at the same time as the wreck of the little plane. They would see what he had written just before freezing solid, my name in his blood in the snow.

STAINLESS STEEL POLES

My father wanted the best for me. He wasn't lucky enough to get an education, he'd had to leave school at the age of fifteen to work in his father's garage, to bring a little money into the family, he didn't want the same thing to happen to me, that's why he paid three thousand dollars a year to send me to the Lycée de Chicoutimi. When I got good grades, he'd open a beer and offer me some, he saw in me a doctor, a lawyer, an engineer, and at one point I almost believed such nonsense, he nearly had me buying into it, a liberal profession with all that was implied: a two-storey house in Domaine-du-Roy, an in-ground swimming pool, a dog, a car with lots of chrome, a summer cottage not far away, a wife and kids. I didn't want any of it, especially not a child, any more than I wanted a woman, I always knew it and my father felt it too, that I really liked the boys who came to do homework with me in our basement. Still, he insisted on showing me how a man reacts, a real one, when faced with the sexual promise of young girls, dragging me off to JR and sitting us down beside a gang of old farts who came to blow away their Alcan paycheques. I knew one of the dancers by sight. She was Anne-Louise's sister, she was in fifth year at the Lycée, I sometimes ran into her in the hallways. Fortunately, she pretended not to know who I was when she came by our table to ask if we wanted to follow her into one of the cubicles where there were no more rules, you did what you wanted as long as you could pay, it was the doorman who told my father that the girls were open, they did it for your pleasure.

When another dancer came to ask my father if we wanted her to do a little something, I could see that he was hesitating. I didn't want him to shut me up in one of those little places. I had a habit of talking non-stop, and loudly, my potato masher never slept, as my grandmother said, but at the JR I didn't dare open my mouth. At the age of thirteen I was both fascinated and cowed by the sexual world as it manifested itself at the strip bar, where the most unsavoury impulses of the old, unfulfilled Jonquière men, beguiled by the flesh of young girls who were totally stoned, were given full rein in the glow of the Bud Light neon sign over the door to the cubicles. One after another they came to make up for years of bad sex by feasting on dancers their daughters' or granddaughters' age, came to see them writhing around a grubby stainless steel pole, the better to block out their yen for the old friend, their longing for their tablemate, a long-time companion and hunting buddy, only once in the woods did they sleep together in the same bed in the camp, on a cold night when the manly warmth at your back guaranteed an erection. Why not feed their fantasies with adolescents in crisis dancing to get even with their parents and egged on by a bent friend with an eye for the cash at the end of a blow job, why not all go there, men, in a gang. The other guy, always worse off than we are, will be nearby to make us feel less guilty and to help us cope with our shameful truths.

It was on our third or fourth visit that my father sent me into a cubicle. This was the ultimate test, the final dose of the treatment that was going to inoculate me against the hypnotic effects of a blood-gorged penis. Of course, I ended up with Stéphanie, the girl from the Lycée, who was calling herself Pamela-Summer. I had no desire to follow her into the little dim-lit room, but her taunting look that seemed to mock my discomfort, and my ignorance of sex JR-style, was a challenge to my pride. In front of the big-bellied, grey-haired monsters who were chuckling at seeing Stéphanie invite me to follow her, the aging morons who told themselves that I didn't know my own luck, that I would remember forever this session in the cubicle, who winked conspiratorially at the dancer, I found nothing better to do than to follow in her wake.

In the cubicle, Stéphanie didn't even try to play the game. We got along fine during the five minutes she spent sitting on the bench, with her transparent dressing gown closed over her long legs perched on high heels. When I saw her afterwards at school and in the street, she ignored me completely. She'd warned me, and I had to understand: she didn't want people to know, she didn't do it for fun but to pay for school for herself and her sister, the Lycée was expensive and their father had been jailed in the States for five years, they didn't have a cent. Their mother was no better, she drank like a fish and spent the little money she had on booze and smokes. Steph hated dancing, but it paid. And it was delicate because, since she was at school, she had to stay put in one place. Usually, the dancers that you saw came from all over Quebec, they stayed four or five days in each bar then they all got into a minivan, they had one or two days off, and started in again elsewhere, in another region, that way the clients didn't have time to fall in love with you, to tail you at night for your money and to cut off your head and stuff you into the trunk of a car— that had already happened. Stéphanie couldn't leave in the middle of the week, she had to attend classes. She wouldn't be doing this for the rest of her life, so she had no other choice than to be very careful about her identity, seeing that she was in Jonquière all the time. She didn't want it to be known outside JR, she didn't want to tell Anne-Louise above all, so shut up about that, if someone finds out, I'll know it's you and I'll rip off your faggy little dick. I asked her if she knew Paule, Kate Dragonne, a dancer who was the star of Jonquière. All the time I was watching the girls passing across the JR stage, I wondered if it could be her dancing in front of me, even if she was long dead. If this girl rubbing herself up against the pole might have, under her fishnet stockings, a dormant penis. Stéphanie laughed, that urban legend went back a long way. Sometimes a drunk, an old habitué, let himself go and talked about it, and that made everyone around the table ill at ease.

My father's treatment didn't work. I soon introduced him to Almanach, whom I frenched in front of him just to get his goat. I know that my father was jealous of my glorious lover, I turned him on intentionally by screwing noisily in the unsoundproofed basement, I wanted to get back at him for all the nights at JR, to torture him by making him understand that I would fuck all the men in the world before I'd go to bed with him.

THE LAMBERTS DIE FROM THE
HEART AND FROM SAWS

Kevin Lambert, with two deaths on his conscience, couldn't bear having a third. Old Lambert died in his chalet in the Valin mountains during a weekend of solitary fishing, but his son shouldered the entire responsibility. François Lambert was found by a neighbour who had a house on the same lake, and who was disturbed to see the old man's lights on in the middle of the night, when he was more of an early riser than a night owl. No autopsy was performed on his body, given his many health problems. The doctor told Kevin that he was lucky to have had his father for so long, given his old man's negligent eating habits and his affection for the bottle. I tried many times to console my lover during the nights we spent together. I tried to make him forget the death by caressing him and making him come, killing him a little as if to free him from his fierce, tenacious sense of guilt, to ease the guilt with orgasms, to swallow it down so it would never return, so he would make love to me again with his ruthless member, with his mind at rest.

We did not lay François Lambert in the ground. True to the request he had made in his will, his son had him stuffed by an old friend, a taxidermist colleague with whom the old man had made a pact: that the last one alive would stuff the first to die. We sat his prepared remains atop the genuine African lion, which was patiently awaiting its moment of glory in the basement. Having seen it with my own eyes, I can swear that the old man looked proud, bestraddling his lion, one hand at his brow to simulate his gazing into the distance, his gaze expertly manufactured with two glass marbles slotted into his skull. That was how old Lambert hoped to avoid the cemetery's dry earth; the hunter would go to join his prey in the taxidermy museum of the Rivière-du-Moulin basement. Kevin, knowing full well that it was against the law to make off with a dead body in the dead of night, to place it in the back of his pickup truck and go have it stuffed and then dressed in a grotesque costume prepared by the deceased himself (a striped purple shirt and silk pants, with a tie picturing animals out of the savannah), sank into a raving paranoia. He became violent because he was afraid that I would talk, that I would denounce him, he felt guilty for the death of his father, guilty for his being stuffed. Little Croustine's nightmares got worse. I don't know if it was due to his ancestor's body being enthroned at the door to his bedroom, but the child refused from that point on to go down to the basement or to wear the bichon slippers that he had always loved so dearly. His father, at his wits' end, faced with crisis after crisis, struck him one night when he had made himself drunk trying to rid himself of his sorrows. He blamed himself for this impulsive act, which exacerbated the child's fear and mistrust just when he was beginning to regain confidence in his infanticidal father.

Gone was the self-assurance that had made Kevin so irresistible. Guilt made him lose his blond hair, hollowed out circles under his green eyes, and bloated his rugged features. One winter morning he threw himself onto a circular saw, its round blade projecting from a woodworking table. Inside his blue stucco garage, his arms and heart laid bare, with one graceful leap he described an elegant arc, aiming himself at the blade spinning in empty air. The target was his heart. To avoid splattering the entire room, he had placed a plastic sheet on the ground and along the walls, easing the task of the policeman charged with the cleanup. It was Croustine who found his father's remains amid the macabre tableau, and he was the one who came knocking at our door to alert my father.

TO CULTIVATE HATRED

I've hated lots of things. I've hated men in general, especially those who write books, shitty books that never go beyond their sad fiascos, I've hated even more the men of Chicoutimi, I can't figure out how their lives could have importance in anyone's eyes, I have no sympathy for those who mourn their deaths, I love it when they kill each other with their own chainsaws or when a woman, lucid and psychopathic, murders one in cold blood, I'd go to cheer her on in front of the courthouse where she's facing trial. I've not liked many people, to tell the truth, except for some writers, certain girls, and a few homos who write wild stuff you can pick up for two dollars from among the library's rejects, madwomen and faggots who aren't obsessed with questions of substance and who strive with every sentence to demolish beautiful things prized for no reason. I've never liked the people I rubbed shoulders with, whom I met in life, I still blame them for not living up to my idea of them, the great things I demanded of them, the sublime sacrifices they were to make for me. I swear it: I've never loved anyone other than Almanach and a few unknowns, especially the dead I hope to join as soon as I can, and whose photographs I've printed up to put on my bedroom door. Kurt Cobain. River Phoenix. Sid Vicious. James Baldwin. Jeff Buckley. Robert Mapplethorpe. My botched suicide attempts give me a pain, those I imagine in my bed at night while the kitchen knife lies gleaming in the pristine dishwasher. I hate my town that is so ugly, so banal, so sad: Chicoutimi that has birthed so many imbeciles and endowed them with a lust for life that keeps them from slashing their wrists when, truly, it would have been simpler for everyone concerned if they'd just done away with themselves.

Ever since elementary school we were taught each year the same thing, as if the teachers never bothered to inform each other that we'd already seen it all, Jacques Cartier, 1534, New France and the Indigenous people, we knew about the Seven Years War and the Conquest, had learned by heart the British North America Act and the Quebec Act and Common Law, the Upper and Lower, the rebellion of the Patriotes, all hanged at the end of their ropes, Confederation, the Night of the Long Knives. History class bored me to death, even more than all the rest. Every year the English won the war and Monsieur Dostie flushed with anger when we said we lost all the time, when we said the damn English cheated, he flushed with anger because it was a question of point of view, but he still recounted the same idiocies we'd learned by heart since kindergarten, the better to forget it all come summer, when school was out and we didn't have to bother about the Filles du Roy and the status quo, and we went out to play in the streets or in the park, in the river behind the Lycée de Chicoutimi, outside history and everything to do with it.

But every year it was the same: we went back to school and history started all over again from the beginning, repeating itself out of the mouth of a different simpleton, it pissed off all my friends and me too. The first time the teacher told us the story, we thought it was a nice tale, interesting and everything, even if there weren't enough characters or stirring episodes. In the beginning we listened, we followed, we liked the punchlines, and we looked forward to the next lesson when we would find out what was going to happen. The second time around, we already knew the story, we predicted the events before they arrived, we laughed at the serious places, the deaths and epidemics, the wars and deportations, we thought all the decisions were stupid: like sending just four thousand soldiers up against twice that many to get beaten in half an hour, we laughed at the French. The third time and all those afterwards were painful, we wondered whether he was making it all up just for us, our super moron teacher, Dostie. By the third year, we had long ago stopped believing in those children's stories. In Chicoutimi, history doesn't happen very often, and that's just fine when you know about all the horrible, dumb things that go on there.

It was in my fourth year at the Lycée that things started to get better. I'd often heard about the Second World War from Victor, who'd been told about it by his big brother, and that spoiled all the punchlines for me when they finally started to talk about it in our class. We were old enough at last—because it's pretty violent, you bayonet, you gas, you kill by thousands of millions, you genocide, you nuke till it isn't funny anymore, we saw the movie but didn't really believe it. It was too distant, too big, too vague for us to feel it, soon I was skipping classes to play around with Alex or Félicie, my two best friends that year, whose desks were right near mine at the back of the class. Almanach's desk was right in front of mine. Usually he liked fooling around with us, but during history class, that day, he was paying a lot of attention.

I backed off from him during the period following the death of Kevin Lambert, which, curiously, left me cold. I found his suicide gutsy and bloody, but after a few days I'd already forgotten my lover and our libidinous carryings-on. In fourth year, I didn't want to commit myself to one person the way Almanach did, for him it was a matter of respect. He tried talking to me about it at times, he explained what it did to him to imagine me, whenever I was absent, in the arms of another, he shed hot tears when I told him about the sex in which Kevin and I indulged prior to his death. Almanach made comparisons despite himself, felt abandoned and neglected even though he knew that I adored him more than anyone, that I would cover all the walls of this horrible city with his beautiful profile and his curly hair, that his intelligence, his sense of repartee, every word coming out of his mouth gave me a hard-on as much as his sex, as much as his hands with their long pianist fingers, as much as his eyes that swallowed me up like black holes. I called him all the time, told him off, reproached him for not wanting me, for telling me that he needed to distance himself, I couldn't understand his whims, it seemed he did it on purpose to give me a hard time when I was at my lowest ebb. I wept, I moaned, I went to knock at his window at night, it was his father who came out with a baseball bat to chase me away. Almanach, who had never said a word about me or about his homosexual inclinations to his family, passed me off as a thief. As he was threatening me, I cried out to Almanach's father that his son was a fairy, that he sucked my cock and lit into me with his own.

One night I got home from my lousy video store, the part-time job where I spent my evenings renting out porno films to wackos who hadn't yet learned that all their repugnant fantasies were right there on the internet, and on casually opening up Facebook, I read a message from Almanach. We hadn't talked or seen each other since the end of the school year, I'd stopped pursuing him weeks earlier. The final history exam had taken place, and we'd both passed. With the beginning of summer, my love for him had turned into fury. My suffering was great, and I blamed him for depriving me of the beautiful thing that was his bed on Sunday mornings when his parents were at the cottage, which we spent sleeping one against the other, making love, the curtains open to let the light wash over our warm bodies. I blamed him for not allowing us to share the summer of our sixteenth year. I hated his rationality, his self-respect, his maturity. I detested him for being able to make such a final, clear-cut decision. I blamed him, yes, for having warned me, but without having made me understand the scope of his threat, his sadness, his disappointment. I detested everything Almanach did to me, and that I was powerless to do to him. I could never say no to him, refuse myself to him. I hoped every night that he would come to me without warning, slip in between my sheets to wrap me round, kiss me on the neck, and penetrate me gently with his humid sex. I was bad for him, he told me, we'd had good times together, but he needed something healthier, more serene, more attentive to him. And yet he was the one who didn't listen. He was the one who couldn't understand that I didn't care about his stupid morals, his lover's whims, his urge to control me, to keep me for himself alone. I wanted to strike him where it would hurt, where it would never heal. To open a wound and to pour my bile into it. To give him back the pain he made me feel with his impersonal Facebook messages, in which he told me that I could come and retrieve my Xbox games, my forgotten clothes, the books by Hervé Guibert and Guillaume Dustan, and the birthday presents I'd given him.

It was past midnight, but I didn't care. I'd drunk two Red Bulls during my shift at the video store, I wasn't sleepy, and I had to see Almanach right away. He had to know that he still loved me. I had to make him bleed and cry, I had to hit him, curse him and embrace him, take him in my arms to comfort him, massage him where he hurt and disinfect his wounds. I took my father's car without asking, sped through the sleeping streets of Rivière-du-Moulin past the golf course, turned right, and took the bridge to reach the Lycée's neighbourhood. Chicoutimi was deserted, it was midnight, a Wednesday in June, I heightened my frustration by driving like a madman, ignoring stop signs and red lights to up my adrenalin, making myself believe that I had the courage to arrive in the middle of the night at the home of Almanach's parents, when suddenly he appeared in my headlights, I drove right into his bicycle in the darkness. The sound was dull, the impact was strong. He struck my windshield, bounced across the roof, and crashed onto the pavement behind the car, which had come to a sudden stop. Lying on the pavement, in the silent shadows, not a movement from his body. I looked in the mirror: I was sure it was him. I recognized his red bicycle, the white shirt he wore in the summer. He didn't move. It would perhaps have been best to take off, to forget all that, my head was spinning and a desire to vomit came over me all of a sudden. I didn't really believe what had just happened until I saw his forehead covered in blood. All one side of his body had hit the asphalt, his face was covered with a wide wound full of sand and little stones that had penetrated his skin. I kissed his lips, ran my hand through his hair to find the source of the blood, which kept on flowing. He wasn't wearing a helmet, how dumb could you get? I tried to stop the bleeding by pressing on his scalp, which had split open, I tried to wake him, I talked to him softly as if he were sleeping in my arms, as happened sometimes at midnight on the basement couch. I went at it gently, then I became afraid, I panicked, I got angry, I cried, I slapped him, he didn't have the right to lose consciousness in my hands, to play dead like when we were children in Des Oiseaux, he the cop and me the robber, one getting shot on purpose just so the other would press up against him, just so the other would dress his imaginary wounds.

A raw, blinding light appeared at the corner of the street. The headlights of a car that passed us without slowing down. A dying child is not enough to attract attention in Chicoutimi. My hometown was murderous. Almanach's killing was passive: I was allowed to be the cause of it while others made sure to avoid us, not to see us despite the cars' pitiless headlights. Chicoutimi was responsible for this accident. It was in the streets of Chicoutimi that Almanach rode, it was the Chicoutimi street light that was unlit along his route, it was Chicoutimi's asphalt that raked his body and struck his head, Chicoutimi that furnished him with that bicycle. The collision would otherwise have been impossible. Chicoutimi organized its space, designed its neighbourhood so that one moonless night my lover would cross the street just at the stop sign I didn't see. I held the steering wheel, but Chicoutimi streamed through the engine that propelled my car into his exposed body. I swear, Chicoutimi: your end is near.

YOU WILL LOVE
WHAT YOU HAVE KILLED

Almanach's accident was a shock for the whole school.
Those who hadn't learned about it over the summer got
the news in September. The last year of high school would
be unique, beginning with a loss, that of Almanach, with
silence in a class where he would have known the answer;
with his absence from the hip-hop troupe in which he
was the best dancer; with the hollow echo of the Chopin
melodies he would have played in the high school recital.
This year would be shot through with big decisions, lasting
memories, it's one of the most important in your lives, they
said. You mustn't be disheartened, help is just around the
corner. Take advantage of the opportunities you have to
come together, to be together, don't be afraid to talk about
it, we're all in mourning, his disappearance is not the affair
of one person alone, it touches every student in your year,
everyone who was with him in a class, even those who
hated him, even those who called him a fag, a fairy, a cock-
sucker, a Taliban, a dirty Arab. Sébastien, who, all through
high school, was the one flaunting labels like gay, butch,
retard, kiss, Jew, begueuk, came knocking at my door for

the first time since the beginning of high school. He knew about me and Almanach. I wept in his arms despite myself.

At Almanach's funeral, they played the "Grande Polonaise Brillante," his favourite piece, the one he performed with the most energy and vigour. An awfully serene piece under the circumstances, much too joyful to mark the death of a teenager; it should have been something sad and gloomy, but they preferred the recording of his own awkward performance because it made him seem a little more present, a little less absent. At school, the circumstances of his death were not mentioned. They spoke of an accident where both of us were present, but following the advice of the policewoman responsible for the case, it was not specified that I was at the wheel of the murder vehicle. Still, I tried to confess, over and over I told the policewoman that I'd had time to see him coming, I swore it, I admitted to having realigned my wheels and pushed down on the accelerator so that the accident would be fatal. Sylvie consoled me, saying he would come back, that all dead children return as she returned, like Sébastien, Marie-Loup, Pierre-Luc, like Croustine returned. I waited for a long time to see him sit down one morning, without any warning, on a chair in the science or mathematics class where I wasn't listening, was just staring out the window at the city streets, the ugly buildings. In each passerby I thought I saw his silhouette running my way.

The year ended, and Almanach never came back. The Chicoutimi cemetery swallowed up his body in its entirety, let nothing bloom or reappear. He decomposed beneath the close-cropped grass where there congregated, indifferent, the toads. Chicoutimi wanted nothing to do with the tragic death of my first love. What his native city organized was more like a suicide. A vast conspiracy was mounted, a complex system to make Almanach feel all alone, to put him to death and make him believe that it would be best to remain dead beneath the damp earth because no one was there waiting for him among the living. Almanach did not come back because he didn't want to. My hometown knew that the child, returning, could very well shake to its foundations the pure and pristine edifice it had constructed, the beautiful lawn and the fence surrounding the yard to keep all vices within the family. All of Chicoutimi's structures were built over a fault patched up with concrete and asphalt. A long, hidden fault, a flaw that the inhabitants ignored, they never knew how to value the beauty of such a rupture. Chicoutimi schooled all children in the existence and approximate location of this break, just to be sure that they would never seek it out, just to be certain that they would be able to avoid it. It was known that this long slash, that this serendipitous structural element could, if one knew how to follow its mortared path, pull down entire buildings, bring to light squalid structures that were built with the avowed purpose of each night allowing a child to die. We knew it shored us up, we knew, in our innocence, how to rise above it, we also knew that, if awakened, it could collapse all our misshapen monuments.

It was not an easy task that you gave me, Chicoutimi, to speak of this fault under the cover of "who I am," to assume this horror under the name of "Faldistoire," to recount my childhoods and their leave-takings, to survive you as one raises one's head out of murky and toxic water. Foreseeing that I would soon have to present humankind with the gravest challenge it was yet to face, it seemed crucial to admit to who I was, to draw near to this *self* you instilled in me; born one autumn day, having lived through your elementary and survived into your secondary school. To tell the future from where I was perched, the better to see you ablaze when, soon, the first bombs would explode. Because bombs will explode. The child of forever after who sleeps in you, the child whom you allowed to cry out in the basement of a dark house, the tragic child, beaten, killed a thousand times, the scorned child that you left, bloodied, at the tip of a blood-red blade, this child whom you allowed to die while you were masturbating over the future it might have known, this child will rise. Death has no sway over the child who sleeps, the innocent child you are trying to crush, the child you are raping every night and who, despite itself, develops a taste for it—he will resist.

He will grow. You will try to hold on to him. To calm him. To punish him. You will try to sit the child in its place, behind the little classroom desk reduced to ashes. But you know, Chicoutimi, this will no longer be just a child. One day he will awaken with all the strength that will have been conferred on him by that deep sleep. And you will love what you have killed.

ATTACKS

It's four in the morning. On my bed, scribbled notes, maps, school exercise books from all the grades since the second, me in the middle of it all, lying down surrounded by half-baked schemes and bygone prophecies cluttering up my room. My laptop open to a Facebook conversation from the day before over which I fell asleep. I've spent the night writing to spell out our plan, going through the exercises, exams, and texts that my mother saved. I've reread my notebooks to review everything I did not become: architect, doctor, zoologist, astronaut, veterinarian. I never set foot on a new star, or discovered an ancient dinosaur whose species has disappeared, wiped out by an enormous rock from deep in the galaxies, I never saved any animal on its way to extinction in any distant land, as I vowed to do on all the sheets of paper with my name in lead pencil at the top, in conventional, well-formed handwriting, its elegant cursive recently mastered. At four in the morning, my alarm goes off. The scene on which I open my eyes is familiar to me: the basement bedroom painted red, two windows overhead, a bookcase full of unread books, the closet and its mirrored door, my film posters and my Jean

Genet cameo on the wall, a portrait that looks a bit like a death mask with its flowered cloth in the background. The lights have been on all night, I wake to the tentative notes of a long, not very good Doors song, I should have put on "Light My Fire" or "Break On Through" to get me on my feet, this one doesn't make me want to get out of bed, *Father. Yes, son? I want to kill you.*

Turning my head, I can see my reflection in the mirrored door. I have to get up. They'll be here in half an hour and come down to the basement without a sound, so as not to wake my father, who is still sleeping. Every morning, after an awakening, always brutal, to a song poorly chosen the night before, the ritual begins again. I wrench myself from sleep, slide out of the sheets, pull on a pair of boxers, I note the latest changes in my body, a muscle that has begun to show itself, a new hair. I think again of the pleasure we had, Almanach and I, watching ourselves have sex in that mirror, seeing him bury himself inside me from impossible angles, we often played at replicating the cheapest of porn films, we sought out positions that were the most exciting in the eye of the other at the moment of climax, and then we gave ourselves grades, compared our performances before beginning again. I approach my reflection to a few centimetres from the mirror, I trace my face's outline with my fingertips. Like Kevin, I have green eyes, like Kevin, I have hair down to my shoulders; I'm not blond, but I've bleached myself with acidic and corrosive products that can melt the skin. More than ever, I resemble my lover who killed himself. I'm seventeen years old, but my body is deeply scored with the clues to an entire life. The lines on my face are too pronounced for a boy of my age. A clairvoyant would be unable to read the future in the lines of my hand, so cross-hatched are they with haphazard nicks, flaws, trenches that randomly intersect and cancel each other out. I pull on a pair of black pants, wool socks, my jean jacket that makes me look like a bum. I'm ready. I'm waiting for them.

I finish my bowl of Froot Loops, it's almost five o'clock, the dead are late and that pisses me off. Marie-Loup and Sébastien are the first to arrive. I keep my cool, there's stuff to carry, their car is full. I help them bring the equipment down to my room, the cases are heavy, we're careful not to make noise because of my father, we mustn't screw up and have him leaping from his bed like in the game Don't Wake Daddy that we all played as children in the Réjean-Tremblay daycare. My father is a paranoid who always locks his door when he's not at home; I've stolen his key and have locked him in. Even if he wakes now, we'll still win out. The others arrive more or less together. Victor and his sisters. Pierre-Luc, Croustine, and Sylvie step out of the darkness to under the street light, then come down to my room. We form a circle around my bed, and get to work. The five cases stolen overnight from the big work sites in the Parc des Laurentides slowly empty.

"Are we waiting for Almanach? He might come back today."

I'm not waiting for Almanach, I'm waiting for the end of the world. I've spent the night reviewing our grade two notebooks in which Chicoutimi was already set to be destroyed. Drawings traced on cheap paper, maps of the city in black felt pen, red Xs; they were already there on our large pages, mustering the catastrophes to come. Place du Royaume, Talbot Boulevard, the river, its bridges, the various neighbourhoods and their key thoroughfares. The tips of our felt pens had known all that. There's nothing left to do where Chicoutimi is concerned. We are dead and its life is in our hands. My friends slip onto their shoulders the backpacks we've prepared. I see their eyes shining. We embrace. This is the most important day of our short lives, we will be forever young. They follow Sylvie to the top of the stairs, into the street washed by the first rays of sun to pierce the clouded sky.

Chicoutimi shakes when the first bomb explodes. My magnificent friends, my dead children, are blowing themselves up at the four corners of the city. Sébastien has insisted on occupying the Lycée. We've tested the detonators and the explosives are powerful, Sébastien disintegrates along with the walls of our high school as the morning classes are about to begin. We've decided to kill the children first to spare them the suffering to come. Every young person who returns receives a backpack full of dynamite and is shown how the detonator functions; we need a workforce to swell our ranks. They'll soon make their way into basements so that the shock will strike the city from deep down.

"Do you feel all right, killing your parents?"

All over town, houses are exploding. I see it on the TV news in the basement, in real time. I keep my friends up to date by texting them the most recent developments, the missed targets, the blocked streets. We're shown the fires ravaging buildings all over the city. A journalist is hit right in the face by debris from a nearby house exploding during a live report in Domaine-du-Roy. Around nine o'clock, when I leave to hop on my bicycle, the morning air smells sulphurous and the columns of smoke are rising into the grey sky. I can see some of them in the distance, over the rooftops. My Lavoie bag on my shoulders, I pedal out of the yard at full speed. I stop at the corner of the street, from which point the bungalow with my sleeping father is in full view. First a fire takes hold with fierce, fast-moving flames that shoot through the joints in the roof and the house front, near the ornamental, mock door that we never use. I stare at the burning house, trying hard not to blink so I won't miss a thing. It burns for at least a minute before exploding. Shards of shingle shoot into the air, debris flies out the windows, which serve as chimneys for the smoke. When the explosion comes, the foundation shudders and falls to pieces. The dust is swept up by the wind, the smoke flies off. The house is consumed by a blazing inferno that eats away at the CanExel siding, the painted moulding and the Gyproc walls, the beautiful antique furniture, the wooden bed, the cotton sheets and the asphyxiated flesh of my father. The light is lovely, I pull out my phone to take a selfie in front of my dark deed.

Get back on your bike, the city awaits you: I head towards Talbot. At the slightly elevated stretch of highway that leads from Rivière-du-Moulin towards Chicoutimi, there's an excellent view. Dropping my foot to the ground for a few seconds, I'm able to count a dozen coils of smoke rising in the distance to darken the already covered sky.

"I can heat things up!"

The radio is on loud in the cabin where Sylvie is sitting. On all the stations, programs are being interrupted for reports on what is happening; a news reader who has just offered advice to drivers is causing traffic chaos. The town is frantic, people are leaving work, they want to pick up their children and flee as fast as they can, things can blow up anywhere, there's no way of knowing. The alarm in the reporters' voices compounds the panic, Sylvie laughs out loud at their absurd explanations; they suspect the involvement of satanic sects, they float the idea of terrorist groups from the Far Left or Right, a source has just confirmed the appearance of a new Front de libération du Québec, another claims that all indications point to Islamist terrorists, a fanatic on an open line talks of an extraterrestrial invasion, the announcers give free rein to their imaginations in their live reports—an action by motorcycle gangs, Indigenous revenge—all the while breathlessly describing the violence erupting in the streets or parking lots in the wake of the attacks, fights begun, you can't even remember why—someone you thought was suspicious, a free space in a car . . . People talk of punitive expeditions being organized to neutralize targets arbitrarily designated as responsible for the terror stirring deep within us. The authorities block the road leading to the Parc des Laurentides and Quebec City, so as to prevent those responsible for the destructive acts from escaping. This is Sylvie's moment. She starts the engine and, as planned, makes her way to just in front of the Tanguay store, where the traffic jam begins. In the two lanes, on both sides of the median, all the blocked cars are pointed in the same direction. People are frustrated, they're convinced that they're the only ones to have had the idea of escaping to Quebec City. They can easily see in their rear-view mirrors the swift appearance of a kind of big truck, no, a snow remover, a large, well-equipped machine with a mechanical shovel in front and a blower in the back, out and about well before the first snowstorms. It's Sylvie driving, she arrives like a whirlwind and turns on her flashing lights, advancing towards the metal carpet laid out before her. She does not stop the machine when she reaches the first bumpers. The fearful vehicles pull to the side, tell themselves that it's perhaps for an emergency, to fix some problem somewhere, or maybe some frantic person is taking extreme measures to be the first to get out of the city. She passes a few rows of vehicles, the sea of cars parts to let her go by, then the jam solidifies, it becomes impossible to advance, there's no more room to move to the side, to get out of the truck's path. Sylvie puts the huge vehicle in reverse, lines herself up between two sedans, brings the mechanical shovel down to ground level, puts the pedal to the floor. The heavy engine charges the cars, they seem light as air when they find themselves hoisted and discarded by the force of the machine. Sylvie demolishes several car bodies, turns some of them onto their roofs, backs up while activating the enormous cutting auger of her blower, which she drives into a big, expensive pickup truck. The metal is ground up into a shower of sparks. Despite all the lovely wreckage, her situation soon becomes untenable, she can't hold the line for long, more and more assailants are trying to reach the cabin that is shielding her from the objects being thrown. She explodes herself amid a fanfare of car horns. The impact blasts the snow blower to smithereens and causes the collision of many cars. Other explosions ensue, thanks to the gas from the engines. The few valiant individuals who have exited their cars have their skin seared off immediately. Some find themselves trapped by the twisted fragments of car bodies, pieces of hot, sharp steel.

I view the whole scene from the roof of Tim Hortons, onto which I have climbed. The daring of my friend by default has inspired me. It will soon be my turn to play. I climb down to pedal to the end of the world. To watch the world burn, I put on my helmet. Everywhere in town people are stammering that the attacks will be dealt with, they repeat it obsessively as you would a prayer or a conjuring. The police, the firemen, the ambulance drivers are scrambling, they keep on closing important roadways, make arbitrary arrests all morning as houses collapse or catch fire. In the Place du Royaume parking lot I see a woman shot down who has resisted a policeman. They find no trace of explosives under her clothes, but they do discover, while searching her, that she is carrying a child. The peace officer fires three shots into her womb.

I ride through a ravaged Chicoutimi on my bicycle with its double shocks, I pass businesses with their windows smashed—people have taken advantage of the disaster to pillage Future Shop and Terra Nostra, we want to experience Armageddon garbed in Parasuco—I zigzag between blocked cars, the drivers enraged, I take some photos of the more impressive ruins and I put them on Tumblr for posterity. I visit the nerve centres of our revolution, map out our attacks, and when I pass a child who has returned, when I see that he knows me, I give him a kiss. We have planned our strikes well. Pierre-Luc, Place du Royaume, 27 dead. Victor's sisters, Saint-Anne Bridge and Dubuc Bridge, 53 dead. Croustine, the high school, 71 dead. Sébastien, the Lycée, 177 dead. Marie-Lou, the hospital, 211 dead. And then all the other children whom we've enlisted, the children who know that our terror is essential. Almanach would have been the most sublime member of our bomb squad. I carry my explosives as far as the house of my late love, into the cold bed where one last time I masturbate while lending an ear to the world's annihilation. The detonations of my brothers and sisters continue to mark the hours that morning, something which, all things considered, gives me much pleasure.

Towards noon, I start to get bored. I'm afraid that everything is over, that our destruction has not been enough to provoke a true apocalypse. I'm afraid that we'll end up, like all other terrorists, failures, people who have not accomplished the half of their eschatological goals. My final destination, the Chicoutimi cemetery, is unusually peaceful, a kind of calm amid the storm. I go in by the big gate. The dark sky casts a solemn spell over the graves, the pathways lined with shrubs, the columbarium where the little boxes of human ashes are stacked up, laid out, ordered in deference to the identities of the dead. The wailing sirens, the city's panicked cries, seem very far away. Their echoes resound so weakly that you might think yourself elsewhere, in another city or even on one of those promontories far from human habitation, one of those magical mountains people climbed in ancient times to implore the gods to send a few days of rain while they sliced a newborn's throat. I approach my mother's grave, her round stone just behind the big tree. Viviane is buried near my grandparents, at the top of a small slope. Just beside her is a huge hole, doubtless dug the day before, ready to receive the body of someone newly deceased. I slide myself into it slowly, I am no longer afraid of dirtying my clothes. The earth at the bottom of the grave is warm, as if the melting magma far beneath my feet is gently rising towards the lawns.

The earth begins to shake. Chicoutimi rumbles seven times, great faults split the ground, and the deeps from nowhere start to engulf its hideous suburbs. At last the apocalypse I've been waiting for, that we've invoked after each of our explosive strikes with each of our triumphal cries, the apocalypse come from far down in the earth's crust, now takes hold. All the trees in the Rivière-du-Moulin park catch fire, the bridges, already weakened by the force of the explosions, drop into the Saguenay, which is flowing like lava. Great craters open up in the golf club's green grass, the earth belches up its boiling fluids. The buildings are soon destroyed, attacked by the blazes their ruins have spawned. A thousand years of history pass in an afternoon. Chicoutimi becomes a ruin, becomes nothing, is thrust back beyond its beginnings. The little white house that resisted the deluge, that became, through its whiteness, its tenacity, and its lack of grandeur, an emblem for every Chicoutimi citizen, shatters before hurtling forwards, pouring down the cliff over which it had been enthroned, and collapses onto the rocks. The cemetery's earth swells, grave mounds open wide like the cocoons of poisonous insects. All the dead return and take the city by storm, it's like an outpouring of joy, so beautiful are the cadavers preserved intact by the chemicals that were injected into their flesh. The living dead of Chicoutimi work manfully to ensure its oblivion, clear away the debris of their murderous city, or go for the throats of the last survivors. Everything vanishes, the false and the true, the living and the dead, what humans have built and nature as well. After less than a day, nothing remains.

When the earth calms, on a hill not far off, a woman, perhaps Paule, perhaps the fortune teller, erect, newly risen from her horizontal death, is seen climbing upwards to sing a hymn to the beauty of the apocalypse. By her side, I can be seen dancing hand in hand with Almanach. Sylvie and Sébastien, happy at last, are making love. The captured snake, placed in a canvas bag for the sole purpose of pounding it onto stone until it can coil no more, until it can hiss no longer, emerges in one piece, is freed into the grass. No mockingbird swoops down to devour it. What we bear within us is too great and the world is too small. Destruction is our way to build.

ABOUT THE AUTHOR

Born in 1992, Kevin Lambert grew up in Chicoutimi, Quebec. He earned a master's degree in creative writing at the Université de Montréal. His first novel, *You Will Love What You Have Killed*, was widely acclaimed, won a prize for the best novel from the Saguenay region, and was a finalist for Quebec's Booksellers' Prize. His second novel, *Querelle de Roberval*, has been acclaimed in both Quebec, where it was nominated for four literary prizes, and France, where it was a finalist for the prestigious Prix Médicis and the literary prize of the Paris newspaper *Le Monde*, and won the Marquis de Sade Prize. Lambert lives in Montreal.

ABOUT THE TRANSLATOR

Donald Winkler is a translator of fiction, non-fiction, and poetry. He is a three-time winner of the Governor General's Literary Award for French-to-English translation. He lives in Montreal.